Cassie Bowen Takes Witch Lessons

Look for these and
other APPLE PAPERBACKS
in your local bookstore!

Sixth Grade Sleepover
by Eve Bunting

Mitzi Meyer, Fearless Warrior Queen
by Marilyn Singer

Darci and the Dance Contest
by Martha Tolles

Me and Katie (The Pest)
by Ann M. Martin

Christina's Ghost
by Betty Ren Wright

A Secret Friend
by Marilyn Sachs

Cassie Bowen Takes Witch Lessons

Anna Grossnickle Hines

illustrated by Gail Owens

AN
APPLE
PAPERBACK

SCHOLASTIC INC.
New York Toronto London Auckland Sydney

for Susan

ISBN 0-590-40388-5

12 11 10 9 8 7 6 5 4 3 2 1   7 8 9/8 0 1 2/9

First Scholastic printing, September 1987

Contents

Best Friends

Cassie Bowen watched the game impatiently. It was taking a long time for Brenda to lose. Brenda was one of the best tetherball players in the whole fourth grade. She'd already beaten three girls, not counting Cassie. Now she was up against Sylvia.

Sylvia was a good player, too. She slammed the ball hard, and it spun over Brenda's head. Brenda jumped but missed. Sylvia let it go by. When it came around again, Brenda gave it a good punch. Sylvia let it unwind another time before she hit it again.

"Hey! No chances!" Pam yelled.

"Yeah! You guys are taking too long," said Stacy, who was next in line. Cassie agreed. She was torn between wanting Brenda to win and wanting her to get out so they could play together again. Recess was getting boring.

"We can play any way we want to," Sylvia said. "Right, Brenda?" She shot a dirty look at Pam, who until yesterday had been her closest friend.

"Right," Brenda agreed.

The two of them hit the ball back and forth a few more times while everyone else got more and more impatient.

"Come on! No friendsies!" Stacy protested, and others took up the chant.

"Come on, Brenda," Cassie pleaded, "you can beat her."

Brenda glanced at Cassie over her shoulder. She made a fist and hit the ball a good one, but Sylvia blocked it. Sylvia smacked it hard, and it sailed over Brenda's head. Brenda missed, and Sylvia hit it again, finishing the last wrap around the pole. Brenda was out. She moaned and moved toward the end of the line. Cassie took a place beside her and gave her a consoling pat on the back.

She and Brenda Bolter had been best friends ever since first grade, and they discovered they were next to each other when the class was put in alphabetical order. They liked to do everything together.

Together they watched as Sylvia unwound the ball and Stacy stepped up to play. But instead of starting the game, Sylvia pointed toward a lone figure leaning against the playground fence. "Look at Saggy Aggy today," she shouted. "See, Brenda. She's got a new dress."

All the girls turned to look.

"Oh, isn't that sweet," Brenda said mockingly. "Ruffles and everything."

"What does she think this is?" jeered Sylvia. "A birthday party?"

Some of the girls laughed. Even some of the fifth- and sixth-grade girls at the next tetherball pole stopped to watch.

"She sure does have a lot of dresses," Stacy said.

"Yeah, I wonder where she gets them," said Brenda.

"Oh, that's easy," said Sylvia. "She gets them at the thrift shop."

Agatha Gifford didn't say anything. She just leaned against the fence and looked at them.

Cassie watched her scrape one shoe on top of the other. She looked up from Agatha's scuffed shoes, to the dress hanging to her knees, to her hands clutching the fence. Agatha was squeezing the wires of the chain-link mesh so tightly that her knuckles were white. Cassie wondered if her fingers hurt.

She looked at Agatha's face. Agatha looked back. Cassie turned away, but she could still feel those sad eyes looking at her.

She felt Brenda nudge her with an elbow. "Hey, I just thought of another name for her. We could call her Thrifty Gifford."

Sylvia hooted. "That's a good one! Thrifty Gifford. All right, Brenda! Thrifty Giffy! Yeah, that's funny."

Brenda smiled widely. Cassie pushed at a rock with her toe.

Agatha had been in school for weeks, but she still hadn't fit in to things. After the first curiosity, nobody had paid much attention to her. At recess, she mostly stood in that same place by the fence. Sometimes she watched the others play, but she never once tried to join in. And she never said anything except when the teacher

asked her a question. Even then, her voice was so small that Cassie could barely hear from the very next row.

Anyway, Cassie consoled herself, Brenda wasn't the one who had started picking on Agatha and calling her names. Sylvia started it. Sylvia called her Saggy Aggy because she was so thin, and the dresses she always wore seemed to sort of hang from her shoulders. Cassie had to admit that the name seemed to fit the sad-looking girl. She thought it might help if Agatha would just smile once in a while.

"Come on, Brenda," she said. "Let's go get a drink."

"I'm not thirsty," Brenda responded.

"Well, I am," Cassie insisted, taking her friend's arm. "Anyway, the bell's going to ring before we get another turn. Come on, please?"

Reluctantly Brenda followed Cassie to the drinking fountain. "I'll bet she does get all her clothes from the thrift shop or the flea market," she said. "Wonder why she never gets jeans? She never wears anything but those dumb dresses."

Cassie had a funny feeling in her stomach. She touched the collar of her secondhand shirt. Her cousin Lisa had sent it. It was a perfectly nice shirt. The pants were nice, too, and they fit well. Everything Lisa outgrew was just the right size for Cassie. Her mom said she was lucky to get them. Mom said she could never afford to buy Cassie such nice clothes, especially now that Dad had left. But Cassie wasn't sure Brenda would understand about secondhand clothes. Even nice ones.

Mom didn't know how it was. Nobody wore dresses

to Stewart Elementary School. Not even third graders wore dresses at Stewart. Just the real little kids, and now Agatha Gifford.

Cassie didn't even like to think about it. She took a good long drink of water, wiping her chin with the back of her hand as she stood up. "Want to go up to our fort after school today?"

"Okay," Brenda said. "What will we play?"

"Let's take our teddy bears and pretend that we live in a mountain cabin and they're little cubs that we found out in the woods," Cassie suggested.

"No, teddy bears are too baby," Brenda said. "I know, I'll show you my new card tricks. They're real neat."

"All right," Cassie agreed, but as they walked side by side toward their classroom, she secretly thought that pretending to rescue homeless bear cubs would be a lot more fun than Brenda's card tricks.

Partners

Cassie liked Mr. Garner, her fourth-grade teacher, because he was always thinking up interesting, fun things to do. She listened eagerly after math time as he told the class about his latest idea. "You'll be working with a buddy on this project," he said. "You and your partner must choose one story from the reader and prepare a little skit or play to present to the rest of the class."

Cassie looked over at Brenda and made an okay sign with her fingers. Brenda nodded and signed back. This project would be fun. Cassie liked pretending.

"Rather than let you choose who you'll be working with on this project, I'm going to assign partners," Mr. Garner said. "I want to mix things up a bit."

Groans went up from all over the classroom. Cassie squirmed uneasily in her seat and crossed her fingers for him to make the assignments alphabetically. She signaled Brenda to cross hers, too.

"Greg Ackerman and Andy Gleason will be partners," Mr. Garner announced.

So much for alphabetical order! Cassie tightened her fingers, closed her eyes and wished as hard as she could. She and Brenda just had to be partners. Surely Mr. Garner would . . .

"Randy Maple and Mike Dixon, Pamela Peterson and Angie Steel . . ."

At least he was putting boys with boys and girls with girls.

"Paul Murphy and Brian Jones, Brenda Bolter and . . ."

Cassie squeezed her fingers as tightly as she could, whispering "Please, please, please!" under her breath.

". . . Sylvia Wilson."

Cassie's eyes popped open. That couldn't be right! She turned and looked at Brenda, who stuck her lower lip out in an exaggerated pout. Then, as Cassie watched, she turned around to look at Sylvia, who was grinning ear to ear. Sylvia made a big okay sign, and Brenda okayed back.

Mr. Garner continued calling out names.

"John Clark and Curtis Johnson, Stacy Dodds and Jennifer Thorton, Cassie Bowen . . ."

Cassie jumped and turned around in her seat. She was so busy watching Brenda and Sylvia that she'd forgotten to listen for her own name. The sound of it startled her. She was even less prepared to hear the name of her partner.

". . . and Agatha Gifford."

Cassie wished she could sink into the floor. She felt eyes looking at her from every direction in the room. Some, like Brenda, looked sympathetic, but others seemed to find it very amusing. Especially Sylvia. She wished Sylvia had been the one to get Agatha for a partner. *That* would be funny!

Looking down at her lap to avoid all the faces, Cassie found that her fingers were still crossed. A lot of good that had done! She had to have the rottenest luck in the world! Anybody in the whole class would have been better than Saggy Aggy. Anybody in the whole school, in fact! Absolutely anybody! Even a boy! Even the worst boy in the class!

Now Cassie was going to have to sit with that dumb Agatha Gifford and work with her every day for at least a week, and then, worst of all, she was going to have to stand up in front of the entire class and do a stupid skit with her! It was too much!

As the teacher read the names of the other partners, Cassie rubbed her fingers back and forth in the pencil slot on her desk. She wondered what the other kids would say. What if they teased her the way they did Agatha? What if Sylvia made up a dumb name for her, too, and they all started calling her that? Cassie would absolutely die if they did!

She hated Mr. Garner and his stupid ideas. "I won't do it!" she said under her breath. "I'll get sick. I won't come." The way her stomach felt, she wouldn't have to pretend to be sick.

She was careful to keep her eyes down, watching her

fingers go back and forth along the groove. She didn't want to see the other kids looking at her. Not even Brenda. She didn't want to see anyone laughing at her, or feeling sorry for her either. And most of all, she didn't want to see Agatha Gifford. She didn't want to see those terrible sad eyes.

Mr. Garner finished calling the names. "Today is Monday," he said. "We'll be working on these projects all this week and, depending on how things go, we'll present them sometime next week. You may use the rest of the time today to meet with your partners and start making your plans."

Agatha Gifford

All around Cassie, kids jumped out of their seats and hurried to their partners. Brenda stopped in front of her desk. "I'm sorry, Cassie," she whispered.

Sylvia came up beside Brenda and took her hand. "Yeah! Too bad you got stuck with the creep." She grinned as she pulled Brenda away.

Cassie watched them settle cozily into the book corner. Slowly she turned in her seat until she could just barely see Agatha out of the corner of her eye. Agatha was looking the other way.

Cassie turned farther around. The girl was staring out the window. Her chin was trembling. It was worse than when the others teased her. Her chin never trembled the slightest bit then.

Cassie swallowed, but she couldn't get rid of the lump in her throat. She brushed her short brown hair away from her face. It fell right back. Her body seemed so heavy, she could hardly move. Slowly she pushed herself up out of her chair. She smoothed her hands down over her jeans and took one step toward Agatha's desk. Then she took another . . . and another.

As she got closer, Cassie swallowed hard and tried to make herself smile. "Hi," she said. Her voice barely squeaked it out.

Agatha was still staring out the window. She didn't even turn around when she said, "You don't have to."

Cassie could scarcely hear her. She leaned closer. "What?"

"You don't have to do it with me. Maybe Mr. Garner will let you do it with your friends."

"That's okay," Cassie said. "I don't mind." The lie sort of stuck in her throat where the lump was, but the truth would have been even harder to say.

Agatha finally looked up.

Cassie met her eyes momentarily, looked down at the floor and shrugged. "Which story do you want to do?"

Agatha turned back to the window. "None," she said shortly.

Silently Cassie stood watching the other girl. It wouldn't be her fault if Agatha refused to do anything. She had tried, after all. She was the one who had come over to Agatha.

Cassie looked up at Mr. Garner. He was busy at his desk. Maybe she should just go tell him this wasn't going to work because Agatha didn't want to do it. Maybe she should ask him if she could join Brenda and Sylvia instead.

She glanced back at the book corner. They were

laughing, leaning close together, Sylvia's blonde braids against Brenda's long, dark curls. Maybe if she asked . . . No, Mr. Garner wouldn't let her do that. He'd probably just talk to Agatha and tell them they'd have to work it out.

Cassie wanted to run through the door as fast as she could go. She wanted to, but she didn't. Instead, she cleared her throat and looked back at Agatha.

"Really," she said, trying to sound cheerful. "Which one do you want?"

Agatha just looked at her for a while. Finally she said, "I don't know. Which do you want?"

"I don't know either," Cassie said. "Wait a minute. I'll go get my book."

"We could use mine," Agatha offered, pulling her reader out of her desk.

Cassie moved an empty chair closer to Agatha and sat down. "I can't remember most of the stories," she admitted. "Reading isn't my best thing."

"I know," Agatha said softly.

Cassie looked at her in surprise.

"I mean, you're a really good reader," Agatha said quickly. "It's just that in math, you're better. You're always best in math. I have trouble with those fractions."

"Oh," Cassie said meekly. She didn't know what else to say. She had no idea the new girl had ever noticed her at all.

Agatha began turning the pages of the book while Cassie looked on. When she came to a picture of a deli-

cately colored bird, Agatha's face brightened. "This is my favorite," she said just above a whisper.

"'The Nightingale,'" Cassie read. She vaguely remembered something about a princess and a bird in the forest.

"My grandmother has a bird like that," Agatha said quietly. "Her papa gave it to her when she was a little girl."

"He gave her a nightingale?"

"Not a real one." Agatha's eyes shone as she spoke. "It's in a music box. You should see. It's the most beautiful thing in the whole world. You should just see it. Maybe . . . maybe you could come over after school?"

Cassie shuddered at the idea.

"Grandma keeps it in a drawer because it's so special, but she'll take it out and show it to us if I ask her."

"I don't know," Cassie said. "I mean, I'm going to be busy today. So I can't. Maybe you could bring it to school tomorrow or something."

"It's okay." Agatha shrugged and looked back down at the book.

She turned several pages before Cassie spoke again. "Well, I really wouldn't have to see it, would I? You could probably do the nightingale part, and I could be the princess or something. How would that be?"

"If that's what you want," Agatha said. "Or we could just pick a different story."

Cassie was sorry to see that sad look back in Agatha's eyes. She hadn't meant to hurt the girl's feelings, but imagine what the other kids would say. She could just hear Sylvia laughing and saying stupid things. Maybe even calling her names, too. No. Working with Agatha in class was one thing. She had to do that. But no way would she go over to Agatha's house. Not for anything!

Sharing a Secret

Mr. Garner called for clean-up time. Brenda caught Cassie's attention and motioned for her to go to the back of the room. When they were alone in the corner, Brenda whispered eagerly, "How about asking Sylvia to go to the fort with us today?"

"I don't know," Cassie said. "It's our secret. We've never shown it to anybody before."

"I know," said Brenda. "But we could let Sylvia come, couldn't we? Just this one time."

"How come you like Sylvia so much all of a sudden? Just 'cause she gives you chances in tetherball?"

"No, it's not that. It's because she's fun and she's nice, too."

"I think she's bossy."

"Sometimes, maybe, but since she and Pam had that big fight yesterday, Pam won't play with her or talk to her or anything. So Sylvia's feeling really bad. Couldn't we let her come? Just today for a little while."

Cassie hesitated.

"Come on," Brenda coaxed. "It can be sort of like a party. My mom will let us make some lemonade, and Sylvia said she'd bring some cookies."

"You already told her!" Cassie burst out. Brenda shushed her. Cassie lowered her voice to a loud whisper. "You didn't even ask me, and you already told her about the fort!"

"I just said maybe she could come. I didn't say for sure."

"But we promised we'd never even *tell* anybody about it!"

"Oh, come on, Cassie," Brenda soothed. "Don't be mad. I just thought it would be fun with three for a change. That's all. She doesn't have to come if you don't want." Brenda put an arm around Cassie as she spoke.

"We're waiting, girls," Mr. Garner said impatiently.

They were surprised to see everyone else already sitting down. "Talk about it later," Brenda whispered under her breath as the two hurried to their seats.

"Since you're the last ones to sit down," Mr. Garner said, "you'll be the last to leave. The rest of the class may go."

For the second time in one afternoon, Cassie felt that the eyes of all of her classmates were focused on her. She'd never been in trouble in school before. This had to be the worst day of her whole life!

When the last student was finally out the door, Mr. Garner turned to the two of them. Cassie sat with her back straight and her hands folded properly on her desk.

She looked up into her teacher's stern face and swallowed, waiting for . . . for whatever was going to happen.

To her relief, the look in Mr. Garner's eyes softened. When he spoke, it was with a concern Cassie hadn't expected. "Do you have a problem you'd like to talk about?"

"No," said Brenda.

Cassie lowered her eyes. Dare she ask to change partners? Maybe he would understand. Maybe . . . "No," she said meekly.

"You're sure?" he said gently.

"Yes." Both girls nodded.

"All right, then, you may go," said Mr. Garner, "but from now on, I hope you'll be more careful about following directions when they are given."

"We will," Brenda said as both girls hurried toward the door.

Sylvia was waiting for them just outside. "Well?" she said.

"No big deal," Brenda answered. "He just said to pay attention next time."

"I didn't mean that," Sylvia said impatiently. "I meant do I come, or don't I?"

Brenda turned to Cassie. "What do you say?"

Cassie hesitated. "Okay." She shrugged.

"Great! This will be fun!" Brenda gave Cassie's arm a squeeze and turned to Sylvia. "Meet us at my house as soon as you can."

"No. I've got a better idea," Sylvia said. "You come

with me. We'll go to my house first, get the cookies and stuff and then go to your house together."

"I can't," Cassie said. "I have to go straight home first, or I'll be in big trouble."

"Well, *you* can still come with me, can't you?" Sylvia said directly to Brenda.

Brenda looked from one to the other.

"Please?" Sylvia begged. "You have to. I'm not even sure how to get to your house, and I don't want to walk all that way by myself. Come on, Brenda. Please?"

Cassie shuffled her feet and waited for Brenda to tell Sylvia no. She and Brenda always walked home together. It was another lucky thing about being best friends. They walked the same direction most of the way, until they got to their special corner. From there, each had just a short distance to go alone. They met at their corner every morning, too.

Brenda looked at Cassie. "We could meet you back at our corner," she said.

Cassie shrugged. Rotten day, she thought. Rotten, rotten day.

"That will be okay, won't it?" Brenda asked.

"I guess so," Cassie answered. She didn't know what else she could say.

"Good! Now let's go." Sylvia grabbed Brenda's hand and pulled her down the street.

"See you in a few minutes," Brenda called over her shoulder.

Cassie stared after the two girls. Then she turned and ran toward her own house, leaping up the steps just as her brother Joel unlocked the door. She rushed past him and headed for her room.

"Jeez!" Joel said. "Where's the fire?"

Cassie didn't bother to respond. She didn't care to waste time bickering with Joel. She had to change clothes. Quickly she took off her school clothes and pulled on her favorite T-shirt. Now which pants? She grabbed the green ones but, remembering the patch on the knee, pushed them aside and dug the red ones from the bottom of the drawer. Better not to invite trouble with Sylvia coming. Quickly she pulled them on and stuck her feet into her old sneakers.

She was almost out the door before she remembered her brother. Mom said he was in charge until she got home from work, and Cassie was supposed to make sure he always knew where she was. "I'm going over to Brenda's," she called.

"What did you say?" he asked.

Cassie stopped and called out louder, "I said I'm going over to Brenda's."

"Whose?"

"Brenda's," she shouted. "You know, my friend Brenda, with the long, dark brown hair and two eyes and a nose and a mouth."

"Not as big as yours," Joel said, strolling into the room with a bag of corn chips and a glass of juice.

"Look who's talking," Cassie said. "So? You've got the message, right?"

"Right," Joel said. "Just be back before Mom gets home."

"Don't worry," Cassie said, letting the door slam behind her. It was a pain having a brother for a baby-sitter. All he did was boss her around. Ever since Dad left, he thought he was so important. He said he was the "man of the house" now. But he wasn't a man. He was only thirteen years old. Besides, she didn't need any baby-sitter. She could take very good care of herself.

She hurried down the street to their special corner. The other girls weren't there yet. Grabbing hold of the street sign, Cassie spun around it until she got dizzy and had to sit down. She stuck her feet out in front of her and moved them back and forth like windshield wipers. First she made them both go the same direction like the wipers on Mom's car. Then she made them go opposite directions so they hit in the middle.

Watching the stripes on her sneakers go back and forth, she remembered Agatha's shoes rubbing together by the fence at school. She wondered if Agatha had any sneakers, or just those brown leather shoes she always wore.

It seemed to Cassie that she had been waiting an awfully long time. She stood up and walked the cracks in the sidewalk as if walking a tightrope. She made it to the little platform on the end. Everyone cheered. She waved and stepped back onto the rope. Carefully, carefully . . . step by step . . . all the way back across. She made it again. Everyone cheered as she took her bow.

Still, there was no sign of Brenda. Cassie began to think maybe the other girls had gotten there first and gone on without her. Probably because she had that stupid argument with her brother. She probably took too long. She peered down the street. They weren't anywhere in sight.

She started toward Brenda's house, walking slowly and taking small steps, just in case she was wrong. She counted her steps as she went, carefully avoiding the cracks in the sidewalk. Step on a crack and break your mother's back.

She wondered if her mother's back had hurt while she was playing tightrope walker. Sometimes her mom said her back hurt when she got home at night. She worked hard all day. Cassie wished things could be the way they used to be, with Mom there waiting when Cassie got home from school.

"Seventy-three, seventy-four, step over the crack, seventy-five, seventy-six, step over the crack, seventy-seven . . ." Cassie heard voices and giggling in the distance. She turned to see Brenda and Sylvia coming up the street behind her.

"Hey, Cassie! Wait up!" Brenda called. She and Sylvia continued to talk and laugh as they approached.

"Been waiting long?" Brenda called as they got closer.

"Pretty long."

"Sorry," Brenda said. She looked at Sylvia, and they burst into giggles again. Cassie wished she knew what was so funny.

"Sylvia was just showing me her room and all her things," Brenda explained. "You should see all the stuff she has in there! See what she gave me?" Brenda held out her hand. In her palm was a tiny glass elephant. "Isn't he neat?"

Cassie nodded. "It's cute."

"Did you ever see such a teeny little elephant? I'm going to call him Sylvester, after Sylvia. Get it? Sylvia . . . Sylvester. Good idea, huh? You should see! She has tons of these things. I mean, not just elephants. All kinds of animals and stuff."

"It's my collection," Sylvia said proudly. "I've been collecting little glass animals since I was a baby practically."

"You've been collecting big ones, too. Right?" said Brenda.

"You mean my stuffed animals," Sylvia said. "I collect just about everything. I'm a real collecting freak. That's what my mother says. She says I'm just like her. She collects things, too. My dad says he'll have to add onto the house just to have enough room for all our collections. But then he says we'd probably just fill it up, too, and we still wouldn't have room to live."

"Speaking of freaks," Brenda said, "there's a real one for you." She pointed in the direction of the Gifford house just ahead of them.

Old Witch Gifford

"Come on," Cassie urged, "let's cross." Since the Gifford house was directly between their own homes, she and Brenda passed it frequently. Not wanting to get any closer than necessary, they had made a habit of crossing to the other side of the street. Especially since Agatha came. Once they saw her face peering out one of the front windows. It had made Cassie sad to think how lonely it must be inside that old house.

It was large, very run-down and badly in need of paint. Where the paint had peeled off, the wood was gray and faded from the weather. The whole house seemed to sag, as if tired from standing all those years. It reminded Cassie of all the haunted houses she'd seen on television and in the movies, and thinking about that always sent a chill down her spine. It was a good house for ghosts, maybe, but not for people.

"That's where Agatha lives," Brenda said.

"Saggy Aggy? It's a good place for her!" Sylvia

hooted. "Get it? It's a real saggy house. Who's that?" She pointed to a dark figure squatting among the flowers in the garden.

"That's her grandmother, old Mrs. Gifford," Cassie said in hushed tones.

"Looks more like a witch, if you ask me," said Sylvia, and in her dark dress, with a big hat flopping over her face, the other girls had to agree.

"I know what you mean," Brenda whispered. "She's definitely weird."

"Shhh! Listen. She's talking to her flowers again," Cassie said.

"Yeah, she always does that," added Brenda. "Listen."

"Now you just stand right up here, petunias. I don't know what it is about you girls. You look like fresh young things, but you slouch over like tired old ladies. I'm the only old lady around here. What's the matter with you? Does your backbone hurt? Flowers with arthritis maybe?" Mrs. Gifford chuckled.

The girls looked at one another and burst into giggles, trying to stifle them behind their hands. Old Mrs. Gifford looked up from her flowers. Quickly, they turned their faces away and, laughing harder than ever, walked on as if their amusement had nothing to do with her.

Cassie glanced over at the bright flower beds. Though she had never admitted it to anyone, Cassie rather liked the old woman's garden. It was so cheerful and orderly, not at all like the house. By contrast, it

27

made the run-down house appear even stranger and more forlorn.

Stepping up beside Brenda, she said, "Remember that time she tried to give us some flowers?"

Brenda nodded. "We ran away. We thought she might be trying to trap us or something."

"Like the witch in the gingerbread house!" Sylvia suggested. "Well, she doesn't scare me. Hey! I know! Let's have some fun. Pretend you're chasing me, okay? Come on."

She took off running with Brenda at her heels. Cassie took a few steps, too, but stopped when she saw Sylvia swing around and head straight for the old house.

Sylvia came to a sudden stop right beside the garden. Brenda couldn't help running into her. Sylvia gave an extra push when they collided, so that Brenda fell headlong into the flowers. Brenda sat up, her mouth open in surprise, but before she could utter a sound, Sylvia said, "Oh, I'm sorry. I'm so clumsy. Here, let me help."

Trampling the plants, she waded into the flower bed and offered Brenda her hand. But just as Brenda started to rise, Sylvia let her slip back into the flowers and, with a cry, fell down beside her.

"Oh, dear," Sylvia moaned dramatically. "I told you I was clumsy. Now I've probably smashed the cookies." Sitting there in the middle of the garden, she opened her bag and peered inside. "No. They're all right."

Alarmed, Cassie looked at Mrs. Gifford. The woman watched speechlessly. Cassie wondered what she would do. Mrs. Gifford just stood there, horror-stricken.

Suddenly she exploded. "What are you doing? What are you doing?" She waved her arms frantically in the air. "Oh, my flowers! All my poor flowers!"

"Oh," Sylvia said quite calmly. "Pardon us. Are these your flowers? We didn't know. You won't mind if we pick a few, will you?" She stood up and began pulling handfuls of flowers. "We need some for our party, don't we?"

Brenda got to her feet and brushed herself off. "Sure," she said a bit uncertainly. She started picking, too. "We need a lot for our party, right?"

Cassie wanted to get out of there, but her feet wouldn't move. As she watched helplessly, a slight movement in the window caught her eye. Someone pushed the curtain aside, and a face peered out. It was hard to see into the shadows, but Cassie knew it must be Agatha. In a few seconds, she disappeared.

Still waving her arms in the air, Mrs. Gifford dashed to the porch, grabbed a broom and ran after the other two girls. She swung the broom and screamed, "Get out of my flowers! Get out of my flowers! You little hooligans!"

Sylvia squealed and took off, with Brenda right at her heels. The broom swung wildly behind them. Brenda glanced back over her shoulder to see it make a vicious sweep just inches from her nose. With a shriek, she threw her handful of flowers into the air and burst ahead faster than ever.

On the other side of the street, Cassie ran, too, but not before she saw Agatha step out onto the front porch.

They didn't stop running until they reached Brenda's front door, where she and Sylvia collapsed into another fit of giggles.

"Whew!" Sylvia said, wiping a hand across her brow. "That was close!"

"You're telling me!" Brenda panted. "She's probably still screaming and waving that broom. Hey, what took you so long?" she said as Cassie ran up and dropped on the step beside her.

"Yeah, and why didn't you get any flowers?" Sylvia said. "Are you chicken or something?"

"I . . . I just . . ." Cassie stammered.

"Well, I didn't bring any back with me either," Brenda said. "Did you see me throw them at her? Boy! I never knew I could run so fast! Did you?"

She paused a minute to catch her breath. "Come on. Let's go make lemonade. I'm dying of thirst."

In the Fort

Minutes later, the three girls were trudging up the hill behind Brenda's house. Brenda led the way, carefully carrying a pitcher of icy lemonade, followed by Sylvia with her bag of cookies and the flowers, and last, Cassie with napkins and cups. As they approached the fort, Cassie dashed ahead and lifted the curtain so the other two could enter.

The fort was a natural hiding place between two huge rocks. Cassie and Brenda had worked long afternoons adding two more walls of scrap lumber, pieces of cardboard and whatever else they could find. The roof was made of tree branches, which helped hide it from any enemy spies who might happen to fly over in an airplane.

Brenda set the pitcher on a little table in the middle of the room and looked up for Sylvia's approval. "Well, how do you like it?" she asked eagerly.

Sylvia walked around a bit, poked a finger at a piece

of cardboard in the wall and looked it all over. The tree-branch roof made an interesting shadow pattern in the afternoon sunlight. Besides the table, there were two large old cushions on the dirt floor and a wooden crate in the corner. On top of the crate, a discarded mustard jar held a bouquet of faded wildflowers. Several pretty stones were arranged around it.

Cassie looked at the stolen flowers uncomfortably. Brenda picked up the mustard jar, tossed the wilted flowers out the door and handed the jar to Sylvia. "Here. Use this. There's still some water in it."

As Sylvia arranged the bouquet, Cassie began to snicker. She didn't mean to, but suddenly she couldn't seem to help it.

"What's the matter with you?" Sylvia asked with a scowl.

"Nothing," Cassie choked out, but the harder she tried to stop laughing, the more she laughed. She couldn't stop.

"Okay, come on. Tell us the joke then," Brenda pleaded.

"It's . . . it's just . . ." Cassie burst into more giggles every time she tried to talk. "It's just that you looked so funny . . . when Mrs. Gifford . . . when she was chasing you . . . with that broom. Especially . . . especially when you . . . when Brenda threw those flowers up in the air like that."

Before Cassie got it all out, Brenda was laughing, too, and then so was Sylvia. All three laughed hysterically. Cassie's knees gave out, and she collapsed to the ground. Holding her aching sides, she rolled over onto one of the pillows and heaved several big, long sighs. Brenda nudged her with a toe, which only set her off in another fit of giggles, until finally they were all too tired to laugh anymore.

Cassie pulled herself up onto her pillow and wiped the tears from the corners of her eyes as Brenda filled the cups with lemonade.

"Where do I sit?" Sylvia asked.

"Here, you take this." Brenda pushed the other cushion toward her and went over to the crate. She pulled an old dress out of it. "I'll make another seat out of this," she said as she folded it up.

Sylvia took the pillow and scooted it close to Brenda. She opened the cookie bag and offered Brenda first choice. Then she helped herself before handing the bag to Cassie.

"This is like a real party," Brenda said. "Isn't it, Cassie? We'll really have fun in here with three of us."

Cassie nodded. Quietly she sipped her lemonade and bit into her cookie.

"Well, we certainly have beautiful flowers," Sylvia said, and they all began to giggle again.

Brenda suddenly stood up and pulled the old dress over her head. She stuck her arms in the sleeves and pranced around the room. "I'm Saggy Aggy," she said. "How do you like my new dress? Don't you think it's lovely?"

"Oooh! Perfect!" Sylvia squealed. "Maybe we should give it to her for a present. It might be an improvement!" She pulled the dark curtain off the doorway and wrapped it around her shoulders like a cape. "I'm that crazy lady."

"Hey! You're wrecking our fort!" Cassie protested.

"Oh, I can put it back," said Sylvia.

"Yes, we'll fix it, Cassie," Brenda assured her.

"I'm Old Lady Gifford," Sylvia repeated, stooping over and hobbling around the room. "Get out of my flowers! Get out of my flowers!" she screeched.

She looked so funny that Cassie had to laugh. "You look like an old witch."

"Right!" said Brenda. "Old Witch Gifford with her broom, right?"

"Yes," agreed Sylvia, "and I'm teaching Saggy Aggy to be a witch, too. Come along, dearie. It's time for your witch lessons. Today I'll show you how to make witch's brew."

"Don't you think Agatha sort of sounds like a witch name?" Brenda suggested.

"Agatha the Witch!" screeched Sylvia in a wicked-sounding voice.

Brenda and Sylvia both laughed until they had to hold their stomachs again, but Cassie didn't join in this time. She wondered if they'd think it was so funny if one of them had to be partners with a witch.

Changes

"You have to take out the garbage," Joel said as he washed the last of the dinner dishes.

"I know!" Cassie said. "You don't have to tell me. Mom's home now, so you're not the boss."

"Well, you usually forget," her brother retorted. "I was just reminding you so you wouldn't get in trouble. You never think about helping Mom out."

Cassie stuck her tongue out at his back as he went through the door. Absently she wiped the last few pans and put them away. She took the bag full of trash out to the garage and was just coming back when Mom came in the other door with her arms full of clean laundry.

"Do you think there is really such a thing as a witch?" Cassie asked.

Mrs. Bowen put the clothes on the table and looked at her daughter in surprise. "I don't think so," she said.

"Well, if there is, I don't think they'd live around

37

here," Cassie said. "I mean, they'd probably want to live in the country or something."

"You come up with some pretty strange notions sometimes, Cassandra Bowen," her mother said.

Slumping down in a chair and resting her chin in her hands, Cassie watched her mom folding the clothes. She knew Agatha wasn't really a witch. But she was weird. Maybe if she wore the right kind of clothes, the other kids wouldn't be mean to her. Cassie hoped she never had to move to a new school. Here she knew the way it was, what to wear, how to be accepted. And she had Brenda. If she had to go to a different school, she might end up standing by the fence just like Agatha.

"Do you think Brenda and I will be best friends forever till we're grown up?" she asked.

"I don't know," her mother said. "That's a lot of time. Things change."

"I don't like things to change," Cassie said. "I don't ever want to go to a different school."

"Who said anything about a different school?" Mrs. Bowen asked.

"Nobody. I was just thinking that I never want to go to one," said Cassie.

"Well, I don't have any plans to move," her mother said, "but I can't promise that it will never happen or that Brenda's family won't move, for that matter. But if it does happen, I'm sure you'll make other friends."

"Not at a new school. I wouldn't know how, and here there isn't anybody else like Brenda. Everybody already has best friends."

"Well, like I said, things change, and that means good things, too, like new friends moving in or learning special things about somebody you already know," Mrs. Bowen said. "Besides, even if you or Brenda did move, you could write to each other."

"I don't like writing letters. It's not the same. Anyway, people say they'll write, but they never do. Daddy hardly ever writes to me anymore, and he promised! He said he would, but he doesn't," Cassie burst out. "I hate it! Everything's different, and it's not good. I want it to go back the way it was and never change again!"

She ran to her room and threw herself across her bed. She looked up at the little bear sitting on her pillow. Her father had given him to her just before he moved away. She called him PeeWee. Now he just sat there looking back at her.

Her mother came in and sat on the edge of the bed. She gently stroked Cassie's back. "It's hard for you, isn't it, honey? You really do miss him."

"How come he never writes to me anymore?"

"He's pretty confused right now, I guess. Starting a new life. I think he has a lot of problems to work out."

"I don't care," Cassie screamed. "I have problems, too!" She picked up PeeWee and flung him across the room.

Her mother held her as Cassie sobbed against her shoulder. "You have every right to be angry with him," she said. "I'm so sorry, Cassie. I wish I could help."

After a minute, Cassie looked up at her mother. "Why did he have to go? Why can't you still be married?"

Mrs. Bowen smoothed her daughter's hair away from her face and shook her head. She was crying, too. "We just couldn't get along anymore, Cassie. He changed. We both did. We wanted different things."

"See," Cassie said. "Change is bad. I hate change. If you hadn't changed, you'd still be married, and Daddy would still be here, and you wouldn't have to work at the bookstore every day."

"Change is hard sometimes, but not always bad. If we didn't have change, we wouldn't learn very much. Do you want to know something? I miss being home sometimes, especially when you and your brother are here. I know it's lonely for you in the afternoons and hard for Joel, too, but I like working at the bookstore."

"You do?"

"Yes, very much. Every day I learn new things and meet interesting people. I was getting pretty bored, with you in school all day. I really needed more to do."

Cassie leaned against her mother and thought about that. Mrs. Bowen held her and gently rocked back and forth.

Cassie retrieved her little bear from the floor, tucked him under her chin and snuggled back against her mother. It felt nice, almost safe, but she still couldn't understand how there could be anything good in the changes. It all hurt too much.

No Place To Go

All day Tuesday, Cassie dreaded the time when the class would work on their projects. It was easy enough to avoid Agatha outside, since she always stood in that same place by the fence. Brenda and Sylvia played near there at recess, but Cassie said she didn't feel well and sat on the steps by the classroom. It was the truth, too. Her stomach hurt as she watched Brenda and Sylvia together, and wondered if Agatha would say anything about what happened to her grandmother's flowers.

More than ever, she wished she didn't have to work with her. Even though she didn't believe in that witch stuff, she was sure she could never look Agatha in the eye again. Not after yesterday.

As it turned out, the class spent extra time on math because so many were still having trouble with fractions. Then they had a science film. It was pretty boring, but Cassie didn't mind. She kept her fingers crossed and her eyes on the clock most of the afternoon. A boring film was better than working on those projects.

Cassie sighed with relief when the final bell rang. She skipped quickly out the door and turned to wait for Brenda. When she finally came out, she was with Sylvia. They were laughing together.

Cassie cringed as she watched Brenda whisper something in Sylvia's ear. Brenda didn't even notice Cassie standing there. She almost ran into her, and then seemed surprised to find her waiting.

"Oh, Cassie," she said. "I forgot to tell you. I'm going over to Sylvia's today so we can work on our story."

"Mr. Garner said we only have to read it tonight," Cassie reminded her.

"I know, but we want to get started," Brenda explained.

"Yes," Sylvia added. "Ours is going to be really super. The best one in the whole class."

"Aren't you going home first?" Cassie asked hopefully.

"No. I'll just call my mom from Sylvia's. She won't mind since it's for schoolwork."

"Oh," Cassie muttered.

"Come on, Brenda. Let's get going," Sylvia urged.

"See you tomorrow, Cass," Brenda said as the two hurried away.

"Okay, at the corner," Cassie said. Bitterly she wondered again why Mr. Garner had to make Brenda Sylvia's partner instead of hers. It wasn't fair. It was already bad enough on the playground, with Sylvia following them all over. Sylvia this! Sylvia that! It wasn't

43

fair at all! She and Brenda should be partners. They did everything together before Mr. Garner messed things up.

As she watched them go, Cassie was startled by Pam's voice. "Don't worry," Pam said. "Pretty soon they'll have a fight. Sylvia fights with everyone sooner or later."

Cassie shrugged. "It's just that they're partners," she said. "They have to work on their project together."

Pam waved and went on.

Cassie started the walk home alone, wishing she really believed what she'd just said.

Brenda and Sylvia would be laughing and talking all the way to Sylvia's house. Then they'd laugh while they worked on their project together. Probably after that, they'd play and laugh some more.

Cassie walked slowly, feeling more miserable with each step. She didn't notice Agatha ahead of her until they were almost a block from school. Agatha walked slowly, too, and looked back over her shoulder now and then. Cassie slowed down even more, so she wouldn't catch up, but Agatha stopped beside an old stone wall and leaned over to smell some violets.

She straightened up, but she didn't walk on. She turned and looked straight at Cassie. Agatha was waiting for her!

Quickly Cassie looked away, pretending not to notice. She looked back toward Brenda and Sylvia. She could still see them way down the street, getting smaller and smaller as they moved away from her. She turned back around. Agatha was still watching her. Waiting.

Impulsively Cassie spun around and ran all the way back to school. "I forgot my book," she panted when Mr. Garner looked up at her. She grabbed the first book she found in the clutter in her desk and scurried back out of the room.

Outside she stopped and took a deep breath before walking slowly to the drinking fountain. There she paused for a long drink of water before crossing the empty playground. She shuffled slowly out the gate and up the street. By the time she reached the stone wall, Agatha was gone. Cassie found a good kicking stone and kicked it all the way home.

When she walked into the house, Joel was sitting at the table eating a peanut butter and jelly sandwich. "What took you so long?" he snapped.

"I forgot my book and had to go back to get it."

Joel took another big bite of his sandwich and tried to talk around it. "What are you going to do today?"

"Nothing."

"Why don't you go over to Brenda's or something?"

"Don't want to. Anyway, she's not home."

"Oh, jeez!" Joel sputtered. "Just when I have a chance to play some ball with the guys. I've got to get in some practice if I want to make the team this year."

"So go ahead and play. I'm not stopping you," Cassie snapped.

"Okay. We can go to the park, and I'll play ball and you can watch or play on the swings or something," Joel said gruffly.

"I don't want to go to the park with you," Cassie replied.

"Look, I don't like it any better than you do, but Mom says I have to look out for you. I'm not supposed to leave you here by yourself, and I want to play ball."

"I can look out for myself. I'm not a little baby, you know!"

"Could have fooled me!" Joel said under his breath.

"Anyway, I've got homework to do," Cassie said.

"So do it later!" Joel pleaded.

"It's not my fault Brenda's not home. I'm not allowed to go anyplace else without asking Mom, and I don't want to go to the park. Just leave me here. I'll be all right. I'll just do my homework and watch TV, and I won't let anyone in or anything."

"If Mom finds out, I'll be grounded for a month."

"Look, I'm not going to tell," Cassie said. "It'll just be for a little while."

"Okay! Okay!" Joel said. "It's probably the only way I'll get to play ball all season. Jeez! I really wanted to go out for the team this summer. Look, I got to run. The guys are waiting. Just keep the door locked, and everything will be cool." He gave her a pat on the head as he brushed past her chair and out the door.

Cassie ducked and smoothed her hair where he'd touched her. She poured herself a glass of milk and opened her reading book to the nightingale story. Soon she'd read it all the way through. It was a good story. It might even be sort of fun to be the princess.

The phone rang. It startled her. She remembered guiltily that she wasn't supposed to be there alone. It rang again. Maybe it would be Brenda, calling to ask her to come over. Maybe she and Sylvia had had a big fight already, and Brenda was back home. The phone rang again. Cassie picked up the receiver.

"Hello."

"Hi, sweetie. How are you?" It was Mom.

"I'm okay," Cassie answered. "I was just doing my homework. We have to do a play for school."

"Sounds like fun. Cassie, put Joel on, please. I have to tell him something about dinner."

"He's . . . he's not here right now."

"Not there? He's supposed to stay with you."

"Well, he just left, just a second ago. He went to the park to play baseball, and I'm going, too. I just had to finish my milk first."

"I'm very unhappy about this, but we'll have to discuss it when I get home. Cassie?"

"Yes, Mom."

"Be careful, honey."

"Okay, Mom. I will. Bye."

"Bye, honey."

Cassie hung up the phone guiltily. It made her feel bad to lie to her mother like that. She wished she had just gone to the park with Joel in the first place. Now he'd get in trouble, and he'd be mad at her, and everything would be a big mess.

She went to her room and changed into her playclothes. She locked the front door behind her and headed toward the park, but when she came to her and Brenda's special corner, she stopped.

Maybe Brenda was home already. Maybe she could

go to the park with her. It would be easier to face Joel if she had a friend. And it would be more fun at the park. Besides, it wasn't much out of the way, and she was allowed to go there without special permission. It was worth checking anyway, so, crossing her fingers for luck, she turned right instead of left and headed up the hill toward Brenda's house.

Spooky Old House

As soon as Mrs. Bolter opened the door, Cassie knew Brenda wasn't there.

"Is . . . is Brenda home?" she asked anyway.

"No, Cassie," Mrs. Bolter said kindly. "She's working on some school project with Sylvia this afternoon."

"Thank you." Cassie turned and walked back down the front steps.

So she'd have to go to the park alone and have her brother get mad at her and spend the rest of the afternoon watching the game or fooling around by herself. The park was just about the last place she wanted to go right then.

Just about the last place, but not quite, she thought as she neared the Gifford house. She was relieved to see that Mrs. Gifford was not in the garden. Agatha wasn't in sight either. Slowly Cassie walked by, looking at all the blossoms in their neat little beds.

It truly was a wonderful garden. Full of dozens and

dozens of flowers. Tulips, iris, violets and lots that Cassie couldn't begin to name. Her mom's garden used to have lots of flowers, too, but never this many. It looked pretty ragged since Mom had gone to work. Cassie missed working in it with her. Sometimes she went out by herself, but she wasn't always sure which were weeds and which were flowers till they bloomed. Besides, it wasn't much fun alone.

Mrs. Gifford had some pansies just the same color as Mom's. Pansies were Cassie's favorites. They looked to her like beautiful velvet. Suddenly Cassie wanted to touch one. Checking the windows for any sign of movement, and seeing none, she moved cautiously across the street. She stepped onto the curb and glanced apprehensively at the house again before squatting to stroke the velvety soft petals.

She was imagining herself in a dress with the rich purple color and texture of the pansy when she was startled by a creaking sound from the old house.

She looked up in panic and saw the door opening— ever so slowly. She wanted to run, but she couldn't even stand up. She seemed to be frozen and could only stare at the slowly moving door.

Quietly Agatha stepped out. She pulled the door shut behind her. At least her grandmother wasn't with her, Cassie thought with relief. She managed to stand up. For a moment, the two girls looked at each other without saying a word.

Cassie finally broke the silence. "I wasn't doing anything. I mean, I wasn't going to pick it or anything. I was just walking by . . . on my way . . . to the park."

"I always wish I could have a purple velvet dress," Agatha said shyly. "Just like those pansies."

Cassie nodded uneasily. It was as if Agatha knew what she'd been thinking. "They're pretty," she admitted.

"They're my favorites," said Agatha. After a long pause, she took a step closer. "We were just making some tea. Rose hip. Granny says it's good for you."

Cassie thought about the witch's brew, but she didn't say anything.

"I was telling her about the story," Agatha went on, taking a few more careful steps. "After tea, she's going to get out her music box." She stepped down off the porch. "The one I told you about. The bird one her papa gave her. You could come in and see it if you want." She stood in front of the porch nervously twisting the sash on her dress.

Cassie shook her head and stayed where she was.

"It's okay," Agatha assured her, stepping closer. "She'll let you see it."

Cassie glanced at the broom, which was back in its place against the house. She shook her head. "No," she said. "I can't."

"It's okay," Agatha said again. "I told her all about you. I told her you were really nice."

"You did?" Cassie said. "After they . . . after what we did to her flowers?"

"You didn't do it. I saw you. Anyway, Granny says you have to feel sorry for people who do mean things like that. She says they probably don't feel one bit good inside. Come on. Please come in."

Cassie still wasn't sure.

Agatha held out her hand. "Really," she said. "She'll like you. I know she will."

Nervously Cassie took Agatha's hand and let herself be pulled up the steps and through the door. As soon as they were both inside, Agatha closed the door and ran off calling, "Granny! Granny! Cassie's here!"

Left standing all alone, Cassie looked around the dimly lit room and wished she hadn't let Agatha coax her inside. She could just hear Sylvia and Brenda if they ever found out. They might even say she was learning to be a witch, too.

Cassie had never seen so many plants in one room before. They crowded the windows and grew in every direction. Some vines even grew up and all the way across the ceiling.

She had a creepy feeling that the plants were watching her, or maybe something was hiding in them and watching. She tried telling herself that was ridiculous. What could be hiding in the leaves . . . except maybe spiders or bugs? Well, that would be creepy enough. Cassie felt a tingling down her spine. She pressed her back against the door as she peered intently into the leaves.

Something *was* watching her! She was sure of it! She could see an eye looking straight at her from behind a large, leafy plant. It stared, steady and unblinking. She stared back, tilting her head slowly, very slowly, so as not to startle whoever or whatever it was. As she moved, a nose came into view, then another eye, a whole face. A man's face was looking at her sternly from behind the plant!

Cassie gasped and pressed tighter against the door, but the face never flinched. Never even blinked. Her breath came in a sudden sigh of relief. The face was in a frame! It wasn't real at all, just a painting of a sober old gentleman in an old-fashioned suit.

Looking around, Cassie saw other pictures on the walls. Some were paintings; others, photographs. Almost all of them looked old. In fact, everything in the room looked old. The sofa was red velvet, worn in spots, with carved wooden claws on the arms and legs.

Over in one corner was the biggest wooden rocking chair Cassie had ever seen. It had long, thick rockers; big, curved arms; and a high back. Its cushioned seat was covered in a pattern of flowers done in needlepoint.

Cassie tiptoed over to look at the cushion more closely. Cautiously she reached out and touched it with her fingertips, accidentally bumping the big chair with her knee. It rocked back with a groan. Cassie jumped. Something brushed her cheek, and she jerked around to face a vine hanging from the ceiling. Her heart pounded furiously in her chest.

She wiped her clammy palms on her jeans as she turned and walked slowly and carefully toward the door. She reached out her hand, grasped the knob and had started to turn it when Agatha bolted back into the room.

"Aaah!" Cassie clasped her hand to her mouth to stifle an involuntary scream. She whirled to face Agatha, with her grandmother right behind her. Cassie stared at the two of them, her heart pounding more furiously than ever and one hand still gripping the doorknob.

"I didn't mean to scare you," Agatha apologized, gently touching Cassie's arm.

Mrs. Gifford reached her granddaughter's side and stood peering down at Cassie. "So!" she said briskly. "This is the wonderful Miss Cassie Bowen! I'm very pleased to meet you, young lady. Very pleased." The woman extended a hand.

Cassie shrank back in spite of the old woman's smile. She looked at the weathered fingers for a long moment before hesitantly reaching out her own right hand to shake it lightly. She was still careful to keep her left hand securely on the doorknob. "Nice to meet you, too."

"I know your mother, you know," Mrs. Gifford said. "She used to come to the garden club meetings, but she hasn't been there for a while. Nice person, though. You look quite a bit like her, too. I guess everyone probably tells you that, don't they?"

Cassie nodded. It was some comfort knowing her mother and Mrs. Gifford were acquainted.

"Granny says you're to have tea with us," Agatha said excitedly.

Again Cassie thought of the witch's brew. "I . . . I can't," she stammered.

"Of course you can," said Mrs. Gifford. "Agatha here

needs help with her fractions. I don't understand the way they do that arithmetic these days. She's confused, and I'm not much help to her, I'm afraid. But she tells me you're quite good at it. You're just the person we need. You will help, won't you?"

"My mother doesn't know where I am," Cassie said.

"You could call," Agatha suggested.

"Certainly, we'll call her," said Mrs. Gifford.

"But nobody's home. Mom's at work, and Joel, my brother, is at the park."

"Can't you call your mother at work?" suggested Agatha.

"I don't . . . I mean, she doesn't . . ." Cassie swallowed. "I guess I could."

"Good! All settled then," said Mrs. Gifford. "I'll get the tea. Agatha can show you the telephone."

Reluctantly Cassie let Agatha take her by the arm and lead her deeper into the terrifying house.

Tea and Math

Cassie tried to stop trembling as she stumbled behind Agatha down a long, dark hallway. They stopped in front of a tall oak door. Agatha braced herself against it and pushed.

As she watched the heavy door swing slowly open, Cassie felt a lump creeping from her chest into her throat. Agatha pulled her inside with a jerk, and Cassie blinked in amazement.

The furnishings were old, as in the living room: a wooden dining table and chairs with carved backs and legs, a buffet chest and curio cabinet, an old sewing machine with a treadle like those Cassie had seen only in pictures. There were plenty of plants, too, but instead of being dark and gloomy, the room was sunny and cheerful. The walls were painted yellow and covered with brightly colored travel posters.

Cassie realized that Agatha was watching her with a wide grin. "It . . . it's so bright in here," Cassie said self-consciously.

"I know. It's a real surprise, huh? Granny says you should always eat in a cheerful place. The phone is over here."

"Thanks," Cassie said as she dialed her mother's work number. She listened as it rang several times, wondering what Mom would think about her never getting to the park. She was glad that at least her mom knew Mrs. Gifford.

"Brownstone Bookshop," her mother's voice said.

"Hi, Mom? This is Cassie."

"Hi, Cassie. Is Joel home?"

"I'm not home. I'm at Mrs. Gifford's house. She says she knows you from the garden club, and they want me to stay and have tea and help Agatha with her fractions because she doesn't get it."

"Yes, I do know Mrs. Gifford, but who is Agatha?"

"Agatha's a new girl at school. Mrs. Gifford is her grandmother."

"Oh, I didn't realize Amanda had anyone living with her. What are you doing there? I thought you were going to the park."

"Well, I was but I stopped to look at Mrs. Gifford's flowers for a minute, and Agatha and I have to do this project together. You know, the play I told you about. And so Agatha wanted me to come in for a minute to see something, and now they want me to have tea and help with the math."

"Cassie, I really don't like the way you are wandering around alone. Your brother is supposed to stay with you. Oh, well, we'll have to take care of that later. You may stay there this afternoon, but I want you to go straight home afterwards, and I want you to be home by five o'clock. All right?"

"All right."

"Tell Mrs. Gifford I said hello, and I'll see you later."

"Okay, Mom. Thanks. Bye."

Just as Cassie hung up, Mrs. Gifford came in with a tea tray. "My mother said I may stay and to tell you she said hello," Cassie said.

"Oh, that's very nice, dear," said Mrs. Gifford.

Agatha opened a door in the chest and counted out three napkins. "Sit here, by me," she said, patting the chair next to her as she sat down. Cassie did so.

"My Agatha says you are a clever girl," said Mrs. Gifford as she moved cups, saucers, a steaming pot of tea and a plate full of cookies from the tray to the table. "She says you are quite good at this fraction business. Is that true?"

"I . . . I guess so," Cassie said.

"Of course it's true. You always get them right," Agatha said. "I never had fractions at my other school. Now I keep trying, but I just don't get it."

"The way they do all the math nowadays is a pure puzzle to me," her grandmother said.

"Well," Cassie said hesitantly, "fractions are sort of like puzzles. They're like puzzles with all the pieces the same."

Agatha looked at her hopefully, while Mrs. Gifford smiled and nodded.

Cassie realized they were waiting to hear more. "When you divide something into equal parts, that's fractions," she said simply. "That's all it is."

Agatha waited expectantly.

"Like a pie," Cassie explained. "If you cut a pie into four pieces that are all the same, that's fourths. So each piece is one fourth of the pie, and if each of us ate a piece, that would be three fourths gone and one fourth left."

Agatha shook her head. "I still don't get it."

Mrs. Gifford pushed the plate of cookies toward Cassie. "Maybe you could show her with cookies, since we don't happen to have any pie today," she said.

"All right," Cassie agreed.

"Good!" said Mrs. Gifford. "We'll just have ourselves a little tea and math party. Something for the tummies and something for the brains. Isn't that a good combination?"

Agatha smiled at her grandmother and glanced shyly at Cassie.

"First a little tea," Mrs. Gifford said cheerfully as she filled their cups. "Lots of good things in rose-hip tea." She poured a little into a saucer. "Roberto likes his to cool a bit first," she explained.

Wondering who Roberto was, Cassie looked around.

"Oh, goodness! Where are my manners? I haven't introduced you, have I? Cassie, this is Roberto. Roberto, Miss Cassie Bowen, a young friend of Agatha's and a very special guest."

Agatha grinned at Cassie. "Roberto always has tea with us," she explained.

Cassie had never been introduced to a plant before and wasn't quite sure of the proper response. "Hello, Roberto," she said meekly.

Mrs. Gifford leaned over and whispered behind her hand, "He's been a little jealous ever since Agatha came to live with us, you know. Has his nose out of joint, you might say. At least you might say it if plants had noses." She laughed at her own joke.

As the woman picked up the saucer of tea and blew on it gently, Cassie looked the plant over, wondering where his out-of-joint nose might be. Mrs. Gifford poured the cooled liquid into the flower pot. "Lots of good things in rose-hip tea," she repeated, "for plants and for people."

"Tastes good, too," Agatha said, sipping carefully.

Cassie picked up her cup and sniffed. It did smell good. She took a tiny taste, then a bigger one. It wasn't bad.

"Now," Mrs. Gifford said, suddenly becoming serious. "We have our tea. It's time for math."

Glancing at Agatha, Cassie nervously picked up a cookie. She broke it as carefully as she could into two even pieces.

"That's halves," Agatha said. "I know that much."

"Okay," Cassie said in her most teacherlike manner, "what do we have if I break each half in two equal pieces?"

Agatha hesitated. "How many pieces?" Cassie said as she broke each in half again.

"Four," Agatha answered.

Her grandmother reached over and patted her hand, smiling proudly. "There! You see how well you're doing? Cassie is a good teacher."

Cassie blushed. "When you have four pieces all the

same size, they are called fourths. So here is one fourth for you, one fourth for you and one fourth for me."

"We have one fourth left over," Agatha said.

"Right!" Cassie said. "What if I break each fourth into two parts? Then what would we have?"

Agatha figured in her head. "Eight, and each piece would be one eighth, right?"

"That's right!" Cassie said. "What if we each ate one piece? How much of the cookie would we eat all together?"

"Three eighths," said Agatha without even hesitating.

"And how much would be left?" Cassie asked.

Agatha had to think about that one, but only for a few seconds. "Five eighths," she said confidently.

"Great!" Cassie said, smiling. "We can do it with whole cookies, too. We just have to think of all of them together as the whole thing. See, we have six cookies, and if we divide them into two piles, each pile is half of the cookies."

"That isn't nice because somebody wouldn't get any cookies," Mrs. Gifford teased.

"Then we can make thirds," Agatha said. Taking over the cookies, she arranged them into three groups of two. "Or we could make sixths and each eat two sixths, right?"

"Right! You get it now! You really do get it!" Cassie said excitedly.

Agatha grinned and leaned back in her chair. "That's because you helped me."

Cassie returned the smile.

Mrs. Gifford was smiling, too.

Agatha turned to her. "Can we show her the music box now, Granny? Please, can we show her now?"

"When we finish our tea," she said, helping herself to a cookie.

Cassie took a bite of cookie. It was homemade. She ate a second cookie and finished her tea.

"Can I get it now?" Agatha said impatiently.

"Hold your horses, Missy," her grandmother said. "First things first, and first we must clear away the tea things. Actually, I guess the first thing was getting them out, then came tea and math, so this isn't really first, but it is next. I'm quite sure of that!"

"Oh, Granny! You make things confusing!" Agatha accused good-naturedly. She jumped up and quickly stacked the cups and saucers onto the tea tray. "But the music box is *next* after this. You promised!"

A Good Idea

In half a minute, the tea clutter was gone, math crumbs and all. Mrs. Gifford had gone through the big oak door. Agatha looked back and forth from Cassie to the door, grinning the whole time. Her fidgeting was making Cassie jumpy, too. What could be so special about a music box?

Finally the door opened, and Mrs. Gifford entered. She carried a small tissue-wrapped parcel with both hands. Carefully she set it on the table and began removing the wrappings. She meticulously smoothed out the layers of tissue paper, revealing at last a small wooden box.

Cassie caught her breath in a little gasp. The box was beautiful. Its top was elaborately decorated with inlaid metal and colored stones and was polished as smooth and shiny as glass. Cassie resisted an impulse to reach out and touch it.

Mrs. Gifford smiled at her as she gently lifted the lid.

A tiny golden bird popped up and began to turn and flutter as it played a tune.

Cassie was enchanted. Agatha was right. This music box was something very special. She was disappointed when the song ended so quickly.

"Would you like to hear it again?" the woman asked. Both girls nodded.

"It's very old, isn't it, Granny?" Agatha said as her grandmother wound the little key.

"Why, of course! It's very nearly as old as I am. It was a gift from my papa. He gave it to me just before he died. I wasn't much older than you are now. It was the very last thing he gave me." Mrs. Gifford set the music box down and opened the lid.

As she watched the bird dance and sing, Cassie thought about what Mrs. Gifford had said. No wonder the music box was so special to her. It was like PeeWee, her bear. She would keep PeeWee forever, too. He might not be quite as wonderful as this music box, but if she never saw her father again, it would be her last present from him. Even if he was sort of a creep now, she'd keep the bear to remind her of the time before he left.

The tinkling notes slowed and faded away again. The three sat staring at the little bird in the stillness, then Mrs. Gifford began to hum the bird's melody. Soon she was singing, and Agatha joined in. Her young voice was clear and beautiful. Cassie looked up. The girl's eyes sparkled, and there was a happy glow about her as she sang with her grandmother.

66

When the song ended, Cassie spoke. "You were right about the story. It's a good idea, and you'll make a wonderful nightingale."

Agatha beamed. "And you'll be the princess!"

"But what about the king?" Cassie asked.

"Oh! I never thought of him," Agatha said.

"What king? What princess?" asked Mrs. Gifford.

"The one in the story. The story for our play has a princess, a nightingale and a king," explained Agatha.

"And we don't have anybody to be the king," Cassie added.

"Well," said Mrs. Gifford, "perhaps if you tell me the story, I can help think of something. Besides, Roberto loves stories," she added with a wink.

Agatha tried to get Cassie to tell the story, but Cassie would only shake her head. "You tell it," she insisted. "You know it best."

So, settling herself back in her chair, Agatha began.

Cassie stared at Agatha. This Agatha was not at all like the timid, dull girl who stood by the fence at school. This Agatha smiled and talked, even told stories. She wasn't a witch. That was for sure.

And neither was her grandmother, no matter what the others said. She was nice—a little kooky, maybe— but nice just the same. Cassie laughed at herself to think how frightened she had been of Mrs. Gifford and this old house. It had been an afternoon full of surprises, and the biggest surprise of all, Cassie suddenly realized, was that she was having a good time!

"You're a good storyteller," Cassie stated impulsively when Agatha finished.

Agatha grinned, and her cheeks flushed pink. Cassie thought she looked pretty with her eyes sparkling and her cheeks rosy.

"We still have to decide what to do about the king," Agatha reminded them. "We really do need a king."

"Maybe some hunters, too," Cassie said. "At least one."

The room was silent for a moment while everyone pondered the problem. Suddenly Mrs. Gifford raised a finger. "I've got it! Now, your teacher just said you have to do a play. Is that right?"

The girls nodded.

"He didn't say it had to be any particular kind of play?"

Both girls shook their heads.

"Well, then," Mrs. Gifford said brightly, "how about doing a puppet play?"

The girls looked at one another. "I guess that would be all right," Cassie said hesitantly. "I don't think Mr. Garner would mind, do you?"

"I don't think so," said Agatha. "Anyway, I'd probably be so scared standing in front of everybody that I wouldn't be able to sing. This way we'll be sort of hiding. It won't be so hard."

"Right!" Cassie agreed. "I'd be scared, too. This way will be much better. You can be the king and the nightingale."

"No, you be the king," Agatha insisted.

"It would be better if you were, because the bird just sings. He never says anything," Cassie argued. "If I were the king and the princess, I'd mostly just be talking to myself."

"Well, I sing much better than I talk. It's okay with me if you do all the talking."

"You talked very well when you were telling the story, and this will be almost the same thing," Cassie pointed out.

"I know what," Agatha said. "I'll be the bird and the king, and you be the princess and the hunter. That way we'll both have two parts."

"Okay. It's a deal."

"Now, we'll have to make puppets," Agatha said.

"Just what I was thinking myself," said Mrs. Gifford, pulling a box out of a door in the chest behind her. She turned the box over, spilling scraps of multicolored fabric on the table in front of them.

"But I have to go home now," Cassie said. "It's almost five o'clock."

"Let's just pick the things to use," Agatha suggested. "Then we can work on them after school tomorrow."

"Okay," Cassie agreed. "My mom has lots of yarn from her needlepoint. I know she'll let us use some for hair and some buttons for eyes."

"Oh, good! Oh, look at this!" Agatha held up a piece of pale blue cloth. "Won't this be perfect for the princess?"

"Perfect!" agreed Cassie. "And how about this for the king?"

With a smile, Mrs. Gifford watched the girls searching through the scraps for just the right pieces.

"This is going to be fun," Cassie said. "What a surprise our show will be!"

Baby-sitting Problems

As Cassie rinsed the lettuce for a salad for dinner, she said, "I had fun at Mrs. Gifford's today. Can I go again tomorrow, and can I have some yarn and buttons for the puppets we're making?"

"Are you sure Mrs. Gifford doesn't mind your being over there?" Mrs. Bowen asked as she put the peas on to cook.

"No, she doesn't mind. Making the puppets was her idea, and she gave us a box of material, and tomorrow she's going to help us. She's really nice," Cassie said.

"Of course she's nice," her mother said, "but she's not a young woman. I'm not sure she's up to a bunch of girls every afternoon."

"It's not a bunch. It's just me and Agatha. She must have been lonely before Agatha came. She only had Roberto then."

"Who is Roberto?"

"He's a plant. She talks to him and gives him rose-hip tea," Cassie said.

"Who gives tea to a plant?" Joel said, coming into the kitchen just then.

"Mrs. Gifford does," Cassie said as Joel snitched a bite of the cucumber she was chopping. "Get out of that!"

"That crazy old lady? No wonder. She talks to her flowers all the time," Joel scoffed.

"She isn't crazy. Is she, Mom? Mom knows her, and she's very nice," Cassie defended.

"No, she isn't crazy," Mrs. Bowen said, "and I don't like to hear you talk about people that way, Joel. And we need to talk about something else."

"What?" Joel asked innocently.

Cassie concentrated on her salad. Now Joel was going to get it, and boy, was he going to be mad at her!

"Why did you go off and leave Cassie this afternoon?" Mom said.

"It wasn't his fault, Mom. I said I was going to leave in just a minute," Cassie said.

"Joel can answer for himself, Cassie. He was the one who left you alone. Well, Joel?"

"I never get to do anything after school," Joel said, "because I always have to look after my little sister. She never does what I say anyway. I wanted her to come to the park with me. She could have played there. It's not fair."

"It may not be fair, Joel, but when I ask you to do something, I want you to do it," his mother said sternly.

"I was counting on you. If you think it's not fair, you should talk to me about it, and maybe sometimes we can make other arrangements."

"I want to go out for the baseball team this summer," Joel said, "but I need to get some practice in. I don't want to sit around the house all summer long."

"I could stay by myself sometimes," Cassie said. "I'm almost ten. A ten-year-old isn't a baby."

"Well, you'd probably be better off here at home than wandering around the neighborhood," Mrs. Bowen said. "But I'm just not ready for you to be completely alone. What if something happened, an emergency, or if a stranger came to the door? I'd worry too much. Maybe I should try to hire someone to look after you."

"Not a baby-sitter! I'm not a baby!" Cassie said.

"You sure act like one!" Joel said. "Ever since Dad left, you're more spoiled than ever. You think you're the only one who feels rotten about everything. Well, I don't think things are so hot either."

Mrs. Bowen put an arm around Joel.

"You don't have to stay home tomorrow," Cassie said. "I'm going to make puppets tomorrow, right, Mom?"

"I'll call Mrs. Gifford after dinner and make sure it's all right with her," their mother said. "If so, it will give you a free afternoon, Joel. I know that isn't much. I really do appreciate your help, and I know it's a problem to you sometimes. I'm going to have to give a lot of thought to what to do this summer. I'd like for you to be able to go out for the team, hon, and have some other

73

time for yourself, too. Maybe we can find a way to work it all out."

"Can I have the yarn and buttons?" Cassie asked.

Her mother nodded. "I'll stuff them in your mouth," Joel said. Cassie sighed. Things were normal.

Understanding

Cassie woke early the next morning and dressed quickly. She was eager to tell Brenda all about her afternoon at the Gifford house. Boy, would Brenda be surprised! She swallowed the breakfast her mother insisted she eat before she hurried out the door and up the street to their corner. Brenda wasn't there yet. Cassie hopped impatiently from one foot to the other. She was much too anxious to stand still. In fact, standing in one place seemed impossible, so off she ran toward Brenda's house.

Just as she turned up the walk, Brenda bounded out the front door. "Oh!" she exclaimed. "I didn't expect to see you all the way over here."

"I was early," Cassie said. "What did you do to your hair?"

"Braids!" Brenda spun around to show them off. "Like Sylvia's. Did you know that my hair is almost as long as hers? We measured last night. Mine doesn't look as long, though, because it's not straight like hers."

Cassie fingered her own short locks. No way her hair would ever go in braids. Anyway, she liked Brenda's loose curls better than the braids. She didn't say so. She didn't have a chance to say much of anything.

As they walked toward school, Brenda talked on and on about all the fun she had had at Sylvia's house. She told Cassie that Sylvia's mother had invited her to stay for dinner, and she hadn't even gotten home until past her bedtime. She'd been invited to spend the night, but her own mother said not on a school night, so they would probably do that on the weekend. She said Sylvia's parents let her stay up as late as she wanted, and if they didn't, Sylvia just threw a little tantrum and they did. Brenda thought Sylvia was pretty lucky.

As Brenda chattered on and on about Sylvia, an uncomfortable feeling grew in Cassie's stomach. Maybe Brenda wouldn't think it was so great that she had gone to Agatha's house. It had seemed like a big adventure, going into that spooky house, but maybe Brenda would think it was dumb. Maybe she wouldn't even believe that Agatha and her grandmother were nice.

While Cassie tried to make up her mind, Brenda kept talking, and then they were turning into the school yard. Sylvia was running up to them with her braids flying back, waving and calling Brenda's name. Cassie decided to wait for a better time.

She followed Brenda and Sylvia to the four-square area and was waiting at the end of the line when she saw Agatha coming through the gate. Cassie turned the other way. Just because she and Agatha had to work on the project together didn't mean they had to be friends —especially in public.

Still, Cassie wondered what Agatha was doing. Was Agatha scanning the playground for her? Was she walking toward her? What if she just walked right up to her and started talking to her? What if she told everyone that Cassie had gone over to her house? What if she started following her all around school?

Cassie stared straight ahead, expecting to feel a tap on her shoulder any second. It gave her a creepy feeling up and down her spine. What should she do? How could she explain?

"Cassie!"

She jumped. It was Brenda calling her.

"It's your turn, stupid! Pay attention if you want to play," Sylvia scolded.

Cassie moved into the square. She glanced at the fence. Agatha was there in her usual place. Cassie couldn't look at her face. Just thinking about Agatha made her stomach feel pinched.

Later, in class, when no one would notice, Cassie did look over at Agatha and wave. Agatha smiled and pantomimed threading a needle and making stitches. Cassie smiled and nodded. Agatha was okay sometimes. But still, on the playground, Cassie stayed close to Brenda and Sylvia and tried not to think about Agatha standing alone by the fence.

When the time came to work on their plays, Cassie and Agatha made up what their puppets would say and planned how they would build a stage from a cardboard box. Cassie stood up and looked around the room. She wanted to see what everyone else was doing.

"Do you think we're the only ones doing a puppet play?" she whispered.

Agatha didn't know. "I hope it will be all right with the teacher."

"Me too," Cassie said. "It's such a good idea. I don't know how else we could do it."

"Neither do I," Agatha whispered.

"Let's just keep it a secret and surprise everyone, even Mr. Garner." Cassie watched Agatha nervously twisting the edge of her skirt and remembered her singing the previous afternoon. If this puppet show worked, everyone was going to be surprised in more ways than one. "Let's not even let anybody know about the puppets at all," she said. "Let's just keep them at home until the very last day."

"Okay," Agatha agreed. "We can practice like we're going to do it the regular way."

"Mom gave me some yarn and buttons last night," Cassie said. "I'll go home and get them after school and bring them to your house so we can start making the puppets." A little guiltily, she hoped Agatha would get the hint that they would walk home separately.

"Okay." Agatha smiled a warm smile that made Cassie feel even more guilty.

As it turned out, though, Brenda left with Sylvia, calling over her shoulder, "See you tomorrow, Cass. We're going to work on our project again."

Cassie turned in her own direction. She saw Agatha

a short distance ahead and didn't even mind this time that Agatha let her catch up. They could talk about their project.

"Hi," Agatha said timidly.

"Hi," Cassie said, a little uncertain herself. "We might as well walk to the corner together."

Agatha nodded.

They walked in silence for a while. Cassie looked at Agatha, then straight ahead again. "How did you learn to sing like that?" she asked finally.

"I don't know. I just always did it at home. I used to sing with my mama and daddy all the time. Sometimes we sang in the church."

"You sang in front of all the people in church?" Cassie was truly amazed.

"Yes, with Mama and Daddy. Sometimes we sang in other places, too, in front of lots of people."

Cassie couldn't believe it. She just couldn't picture such a shy person in front of a large group. Maybe it was different when she was with her parents. "Do you still sing with them?"

Agatha looked at her feet and shook her head. "They're dead now."

"Oh, I'm sorry." Cassie didn't know what else to say. She'd never known anyone who had died. "Is that why you came to live with your grandmother?"

Agatha nodded. "I used to live with my big sister after Mama and Daddy got killed, but now she's going back to college. She has to work and go to school, so I'm living with Granny."

"How did your parents die?" It was even hard for

Cassie to say the word *die* when she knew she was talking about real people . . . about somebody's parents.

"In a car accident," Agatha said quietly. "They were going to get my sister from college to come home for the summer."

"Last summer?"

"Yes. They got killed on the way there."

"You must miss them a lot," Cassie said.

Agatha nodded.

"Do you miss your sister, too?"

Agatha nodded again. "I'll still get to see her sometimes, though. She'll come for some of the holidays like she did with . . . like she did before."

They took a few more silent steps before Cassie spoke again. "I miss my dad, too. He's not dead, but he moved far away last year, and I never get to see him anymore."

Agatha nodded to that, too. "You still have your mother, though, right?"

"Yes, and my brother," Cassie said. "And you have your grandma. She's really nice."

"Yes, but I still miss my mom and dad," Agatha said quietly.

"I know," Cassie said, taking her hand. "Moms and dads should never go away or die or anything, not till they're old, old, old."

Agatha squeezed her hand.

"Much older than your grandmother," Cassie added.

They walked hand in hand to the corner. "I just have to get the yarn and stuff. Then I'll be right over," Cassie said.

"I could just wait here," Agatha suggested hesitantly.

"Well . . ." Cassie was taken by surprise. "If your grandmother won't mind, you could come with me."

"It won't take very long, will it?"

Cassie shook her head. "Just a minute to grab the bag. The stuff is all ready."

"Okay, then, let's hurry."

Cassie found the door unlocked when they got to her house. "Don't mind my brother," she apologized. "He can be pretty rude. Come on," she said as she headed straight for her room. "He's in the kitchen."

"This is a nice room," Agatha said, when they were inside.

Cassie picked up the bag of scraps and started toward the door, but she stopped and looked at Agatha. She picked up PeeWee and held him out for Agatha to see. "My dad gave this to me just before he left. Sometimes I'm so angry I think I hate him. Sometimes I miss Daddy so much I just want to cry and hold my bear."

Agatha stroked the toy. "I know."

Cassie looked at her. Agatha really understood. Brenda always said she wished Cassie would stop talking about it all the time. Cassie put PeeWee back on the bed. "Come on, let's get going."

A Shopping Trip

In minutes, the two of them were running up the Giffords' front steps and racing through the door. "Ho there! Hold your horses!" Mrs. Gifford said. "Where's the fire?"

The girls giggled, trying to catch their breath.

"I went to Cassie's house with her to get the yarn," Agatha said. "We hurried so I wouldn't be late."

"Oh, I see." Her grandmother nodded. She turned to Cassie. "And you changed into your playclothes?"

Cassie looked down at her jeans. "No. I only have to put on my old jeans if I'm going to play in the dirt or something. I can wear my school jeans for making puppets."

"Do you always wear jeans to school?" Mrs. Gifford inquired.

"I told you, Granny," Agatha said. "All the girls do at this school."

Cassie nodded. "Didn't they wear jeans at your old school?"

"It was a church school," Agatha said. "We had to wear dresses."

"But here, everyone wears jeans?" Mrs. Gifford repeated. Both girls nodded.

"I guess I'm pretty behind the times at that," the old woman said. "It's just that in my day, girls always wore dresses to school." Mrs. Gifford studied Cassie thoughtfully. "Cassie," she said. "What's your mother's phone number at work?" She reached for the phone as she spoke.

Puzzled, Cassie quoted the number as Mrs. Gifford dialed.

"Hello? May I speak with Jean Bowen, please? Yes, this is Amanda Gifford, and I was wondering if my granddaughter and I might take Cassie along on a little shopping expedition this afternoon. Yes, we need her advice as a fashion consultant. Oh, good! Thank you very much. Oh, since I'm not sure what time we'll get back, would it be all right if she has supper with us? Fine, thanks again. I'll see that she gets home safely. Bye-bye now."

As she spoke, Agatha's eyes got big, and her mouth dropped open. Cassie was equally surprised. By the time Mrs. Gifford hung up the phone, Agatha was practically bursting.

"Now, Granny?" she screeched. "We're going to get me some jeans right now?"

"No time like the present," her grandmother said, her eyes twinkling, "and we'd better hurry if you want to have time to work on those puppets later. Just let me straighten my hair."

At the shopping center, the girls led Mrs. Gifford to a store with a good selection of jeans. Agatha picked out two pairs with Cassie's approval, and they headed for the dressing room. Cassie stopped outside the door, but Agatha reached for her hand. "No, you come, too," she said.

In the dressing room, Agatha removed her shoes and pulled on a neat pair of corduroy pants. She held up the skirt of her dress, trying to see what they looked like. "I can't wear these with dresses." She laughed. "I'll need to try on shirts, too."

So out the three went to find the shirts. Agatha knew just what she wanted.

Back in the dressing room, she tried on her new outfit.

"You look nice," Cassie said, and it was true. Agatha looked as nice as any girl in school. In the jeans, she didn't look so thin, and with that happy face, well, anybody would like her, Cassie thought.

Mrs. Gifford smiled and nodded her approval, too. "Very stylish," she said. "Now try the other things."

Agatha did, and all agreed that the second outfit looked just as good. "Oh, I don't know which one I like better," Agatha said.

"That's no problem," said her grandmother. "We'll take them both."

Agatha hugged her so energetically that she almost knocked her over.

"Now, now, no need to carry on." Mrs. Gifford smiled and patted Agatha's arm.

"Well, I don't know about you girls, but I'm hungry. We rushed out without our afternoon snack. What would you say to an early supper before we go back home?"

"Hamburgers!" Agatha said. "No, pizza! Which do you like, Cassie?"

"Pizza," Cassie said.

"All right," said Mrs. Gifford. "Pizza it is."

"What's your favorite kind?" Agatha asked as she changed back into her dress.

"Pastrami and olive," Cassie said.

"Mine, too!" said Agatha.

"You two are making me hungry," said Mrs. Gifford. "Hurry, Agatha, or you may have to carry me to the pizza parlor."

The girls laughed. They chatted happily together while Agatha's grandmother paid for the new clothes, and more on the way to the pizza parlor and all through their meal.

Back at the Giffords' home, they got out the fabric and yarn, and Mrs. Gifford helped them cut and begin sewing their puppets. Their work was interrupted by an occasional cry of "Ouch!" followed by fits of giggles as one or the other pricked a finger.

An Apology

Thursday, Cassie was on the playground with Brenda and Sylvia when Agatha came through the gate in her new clothes. Cassie waved but stayed in the four-square game, and Agatha went to her usual place by the fence.

"Look at that," Brenda said. "Saggy Aggy's got some new clothes."

"What's she trying to do?" Sylvia mocked. "Act like a normal person?"

"She is a normal person," Cassie said.

"Of course, *you'd* think so," Sylvia said.

Cassie slammed the ball into her square, catching Sylvia by surprise.

"Brat!" Sylvia sneered.

"Come on, you guys," said Brenda. "We're all three friends, aren't we?"

"Sure," Sylvia said with a phony half-smile.

Cassie shrugged and served the ball.

By the end of the day, she was actually looking forward to going back to the Gifford house and was glad to see Brenda and Sylvia climb into the car with Sylvia's mother.

She quickly caught up with Agatha. They both smiled, but neither spoke for a few minutes. Cassie was surprised by this awkwardness.

"Why did you just stand by the fence again?" she asked finally.

Agatha shrugged. "I didn't know if you'd want me to come over. I don't think your friends like me."

"That's just because they don't know you really," Cassie said. "As soon as they get to know you, they'll like you. Especially Brenda. She's been my best friend ever since first grade. Now we can all be friends—I mean, as soon as she gets to know you better. So promise me you won't just stay by the fence tomorrow. Okay?"

Agatha nodded but still seemed doubtful.

"I have to empty the dishwasher before I go to your house today, so I'd better just meet you there," Cassie said at the corner. "I'll hurry." Cassie waved and started to run as the two separated.

She finished her job quickly and was soon on her way to the Gifford house. She skipped along, thinking about whether she should use red or orange yarn for the king's hair. Agatha was using black for the princess.

When she reached the corner, Cassie was surprised to see Brenda running toward her. Her first impulse was to hide, but it was too late. Brenda had already seen her.

"Hi, Cassie!"

"Hi."

Brenda stopped beside her. She had obviously been running hard. "Oh," she panted, "I'm all out of breath."

"I thought you went over to Sylvia's," Cassie said.

"No. Her mom just drove me home. Sylvia had a dentist appointment."

"Oh."

"I was going over to your house. Look! I've got this neat game." Brenda pulled a box out of the pack she was carrying.

"Umm," said Cassie.

"My grandma sent it in the mail. It was there when I got home today."

Cassie nodded. "That's nice."

"Well, do you want to take it up to the fort or something?"

"I can't."

"Okay, then, let's play it at your house," Brenda suggested.

"I can't today," Cassie repeated. "I'm busy."

"Doing what?"

"I have to work on my play."

"Your play? You mean with Saggy Aggy?" Brenda made a face.

Cassie shrugged. "I can't help it if she's my partner."

"I know, but you can just work on it in school, can't you?"

"There's something we have to do at home," Cassie said.

"Hey, you're kidding, right? You aren't really going

over to that old witch's house, are you? Is that where you're going?"

"She's not a witch," Cassie said defensively. "She's just like everybody else."

"How would you know?"

"She bought jeans for Agatha so she could dress like everybody else."

"So. They could just be trying to fool everybody."

"No, they're not."

"How come you're so sure about her, all of a sudden?"

Cassie cringed. "I went there, and I talked to her."

"You're kidding!" Brenda exclaimed in disbelief.

Cassie looked at her feet. Then, remembering the tea and math party, she smiled to herself.

"What's so funny?" Brenda demanded. "Oh, I get it. You were teasing, right?"

Cassie shook her head. "Mrs. Gifford calls this plant Roberto, and she says he's jealous since Agatha came." She chuckled.

"That *is* crazy!" Brenda said scornfully.

"No, it's not. It's funny. If you'd been there . . ."

"Oh, no! Not me! I wouldn't go into that place! You're lucky to get out alive, I bet. I wouldn't go back there if I were you."

"I have to. We're doing something for our play. Mrs. Gifford is helping us."

"Do it tomorrow, then. Mr. Garner says we have till next week."

"I know," Cassie said, "but . . ."

90

"Come on," Brenda pleaded. "Let's go to the fort today. Just the two of us. Come on, Cassie, please?"

"I told my mom and my brother I was going there."

"So you can tell them you changed your mind. You can call them from my house, or we'll go back and tell your brother."

"I told Agatha I'd be there today," Cassie said quietly.

"So? Who cares about her, anyway? Tell her you can't come. Just call her up from my house. They do have a phone, don't they? Tell her your mother won't let you. Come on, Cassie."

"I don't know," Cassie said doubtfully. "It doesn't seem fair."

"So? What about me? I won't have anybody to play with if you go over to that creepy house. Come on, please?"

Cassie started walking. Brenda walked beside her, waiting for an answer. Cassie couldn't say yes, and she couldn't say no. The silence grew longer and more uncomfortable. If she said no, Brenda would be mad. That would be awful. They *were* best friends. Maybe Brenda was right.

But then . . . she had promised Agatha. Agatha was waiting. Besides, Agatha was nice, no matter what Brenda and Sylvia said, and more than that, Cassie *wanted* to go back there.

If only Agatha and Brenda could get to know each other, there wouldn't be any problem. They could all be friends, just like she'd told Agatha.

They walked on, getting closer and closer to the Gifford house. Cassie had to say something, but she still couldn't give an answer.

"You should see what it's like inside that house," she said finally. "Plants all over the place and pictures and stuff."

"So? What's so special about that?"

"Really, it's neat. It's fun in there," Cassie said, "and Mrs. Gifford has this beautiful music box that her papa gave her when she was a little girl. Then he died. It's so beautiful. It even dances."

Brenda twirled her finger beside her head, making the cuckoo sign. "Sure," she scoffed. "A music box that dances. You say they aren't witches, but I think they must have put a spell on you if you believe in dancing music boxes."

"Not the box, silly! The bird! The bird inside it dances. It's . . . oh, I can't tell you about it. You'd have to see it for yourself."

Cassie stopped and turned to Brenda excitedly. "That's it! You can go there with me!"

"Me? To the witch's house? You must be kidding!"

"I told you, she's not a witch," Cassie objected. "She's very nice. She'd never hurt anybody."

"She might be nice to you, but not to me," Brenda protested. "I wouldn't call all that screaming and chasing us with a broom nice!"

"Yes, but you can't blame her for that. We deserved it, after what we did to her flowers. Anyway, she was nice to me yesterday and the day before, too. Very nice."

"Well, you didn't do anything to her flowers. That was just me and Sylvia."

"You could say you're sorry. You could tell her you won't ever do it again," Cassie suggested.

"Why would I want to do that?"

"So you could go over there with me and see the music box and see for yourself how nice she is, and funny. She says really funny things, and you can see inside the house and everything."

"What if I don't want to?"

"If you'll go, then we'll just stay for a little while. After that, I'll go to the fort with you," Cassie bargained.

Brenda thought about it a minute. "Promise?"

"Cross my heart."

"All right," agreed Brenda, "but if she starts screaming and going for her broom, I'm getting out of there fast!"

"She won't," Cassie said with confidence, but as they approached the big old house, she began to have doubts. Brenda and Sylvia had behaved very badly. They weren't nice to Agatha at school either, and she couldn't really blame Mrs. Gifford if she didn't want to forgive them.

But all that was mostly Sylvia's fault. And when Mrs. Gifford saw how nice Brenda was, she'd recognize that right away, and she'd like her and forgive her.

Agatha would, too, Cassie reassured herself. And when Brenda saw what Agatha was like at home—nice, and fun to be with—well, she'd like her, too. Then they could invite Agatha to go up to the fort with them the way they had invited Sylvia.

Cassie crossed her fingers. She felt Brenda clinging tightly to her other hand as they walked up to the porch. "Be sure to be nice to Agatha," she whispered.

"I will!" Brenda said harshly. "You don't have to tell me everything."

Cassie took a deep breath and knocked on the door. She heard quick footsteps, and the door swung open.

"Hi, Cassie," Agatha said cheerfully, but her smile faded when she saw that Cassie wasn't alone. She looked timidly from one girl to the other.

"I brought Brenda to see the music box," Cassie explained. "I wanted her to meet your grandmother. I . . . I just wanted her to see how nice you both are."

Agatha didn't respond. She stood in the doorway looking at them.

"She's sorry about the flowers and all that," Cassie said, indicating the damaged area with a nod. "Aren't you?"

Brenda nodded. "Yes. Anyway, it was Sylvia's idea. She's the one who knocked me down and did most of it."

Agatha looked skeptically at Brenda, but stepped back to let the two visitors enter the house. Carefully closing the door behind them, she started across the gloomy living room to the hall. Cassie, still holding Brenda's hand, stayed right behind her.

Brenda pressed up close to Cassie and whispered, "Sure looks like a witch's house to me."

"Just this room," Cassie whispered back.

When they entered the dining room, Cassie watched Brenda's face for the look of surprise and was not disappointed. Brenda stared at the big, bright room, apparently unable to believe her eyes. "See!" Cassie whispered. "Didn't I tell you?"

Mrs. Gifford was entering from the kitchen. "Hello, Cassie," she called cheerfully. "Oh, we have more company today." She, too, looked dubiously at Brenda.

"This is Brenda," Cassie said, pulling her friend closer. "She wants to tell you something."

Brenda looked awkwardly at Cassie. "Go on," Cassie urged, "about the flowers. It's all right."

Brenda stared at the floor. "I'm sorry we hurt your flowers the other day," she mumbled.

"Yes, the flowers, dear things," Mrs. Gifford said, shaking her head sadly. "Well, I'm quite sure you won't ever do it again, will you?" she said sternly. "Since you are Cassie's friend, we'll just let bygones be bygones."

Brenda nodded.

"I told her about your music box," Cassie said. "At least I tried to tell her, but it's hard to describe."

"Well, we'll just have to show her, then, won't we? It's still here on the buffet from yesterday—I couldn't bear to hide it away again so soon." Mrs. Gifford picked up the music box and set it on the table. "Come on, come on, sit down, girls. Don't be bashful." She motioned them toward the chairs with her hand.

Cassie scooted to a chair in between Agatha and Brenda. When all three were seated, Mrs. Gifford lifted the lid of the little box. The golden bird began to sing.

Cassie took her eyes off him long enough to glance at Brenda. She liked it! Brenda was just as enchanted with the little bird as everyone else. Cassie's uncomfortable feelings about bringing her friend along began to disappear. Inviting Brenda was a good idea. Everything was going to work out just fine, Cassie told herself.

Four for Tea

As soon as the music stopped, Mrs. Gifford smiled at the three of them. "Well, I haven't had this much company in a long time. We'll just have to have ourselves another tea party. But we'll leave out the math this time, if you don't mind." She winked at Cassie. "You're very clever, my dear, but all those crumbs!"

"I don't mind," Cassie said quickly.

"Oh, my goodness!" exclaimed Mrs. Gifford, jumping up from the table. "Agatha! We forgot the last pan of cookies! They'll be burned to a crisp!"

She ran from the room with Agatha at her heels. When they had gone, Brenda reached out and stroked the lovely box.

"See? Didn't I tell you?" Cassie whispered.

Brenda shrugged.

"She's not a witch, is she?"

"How should I know?" Brenda said. "You can't really prove it, can you?"

Before Cassie could reply, the woman scurried back into the room. "Saved! They'll be a little extra crispy, but still good," she said as she lifted the music box off the table and set it on the buffet chest. She opened a door in the chest and pulled out a fancy lace tablecloth.

When she spread it on the table, Cassie could see several places where it had been neatly mended. Near the center was one particularly large, dark stain.

"Oh, toad-frogs and catalogues! I forgot all about that dreadful stain!" Mrs. Gifford exclaimed. "We can't have that showing, now, can we?"

"Maybe Roberto could sit on it," Cassie suggested.

"There's an idea," Mrs. Gifford said, "but he might feel too self-conscious about it. Maybe a vase of flowers. Yes, flowers would be just the thing for a tea party."

Picking up her scissors, she hurried out the side door to the garden.

"Who's Roberto?" Brenda asked when they were alone again.

"This is," Cassie said, indicating the plant on the windowsill. "Brenda, I'd like you to meet Roberto. Roberto, Brenda Bolter. You remember, I told you about him. He's the one who is jealous of Agatha."

"Oh, that dumb stuff," Brenda said.

"Shhh!" Cassie said, only half teasing. "You might hurt his feelings."

Agatha came in and set a plate full of homemade cookies on the table. She opened a drawer in the chest and counted out four napkins. As she pushed the drawer shut, she lovingly fingered the design on the top of the music box.

"Why don't you play it again?" Brenda suggested.

Agatha jerked her hand back. "Oh, no! Only Granny plays it."

"It wouldn't hurt anything," Brenda said, reaching for the box herself.

Agatha snatched it out of reach. "No!" she insisted, putting her grandmother's treasure behind her back. Her eyes flashed defiantly at Brenda as the two glared at one another.

Cassie didn't know what to do. She looked from one to the other, wishing she had never thought of bringing Brenda to the Giffords'.

Mrs. Gifford returned with a large bunch of flowers. She took a vase from the shelf and handed it to Cassie along with the flowers. "Come on into the kitchen, dear, and you can take care of these while I brew the tea."

Brenda followed closely and whispered in Cassie's ear, "Brew?"

Cassie gave her a stern look as she arranged the flowers in the vase.

Agatha pulled a stool up to the cupboard and began setting out the cups and saucers. Brenda picked up a couple of them and carried them into the dining room. Cassie finished her flower arranging and stepped back to admire her work.

"Lovely, Cassie," said Mrs. Gifford. "I think we're all set." She picked up the steaming teapot, and Cassie followed her into the dining room with the flowers.

"Quite effective," she said as Cassie placed the vase on the stain.

They all took seats around the table, and Mrs. Gifford poured tea into their cups. "How nicely you've arranged everything, girls. Help yourself, Brenda, dear," she said, passing the plate of cookies to her newest guest. "Tell me, are you going to be the king now?"

"King?" said Brenda in a puzzled tone.

Agatha looked confused, too. So did Cassie for a few seconds, but she was the first to understand the mix-up. "Oh, no. She's not in our play. She's doing one with another girl."

"Ours is just Cassie and me," Agatha said, smiling tentatively at Cassie.

Cassie returned the smile, glad to see that Agatha wasn't still upset with her for bringing Brenda along.

"I was in a play once," Mrs. Gifford said. "I was a flower fairy, dressed in a yellow gown, and I had to dance all around the stage. Just about your age, too."

Cassie tried to imagine Mrs. Gifford as a little girl in a yellow fairy costume. She pictured her with a flower crown and long, flowing hair. "I'll bet you were pretty," she said.

"It's probably hard for you to imagine I was ever a little girl," said Mrs. Gifford.

"Were lots of people watching?" Agatha asked.

"Just about everybody in town, I suppose," her grandmother said.

"I'd be scared. I'll be scared just in front of our

class," Cassie said. "I'd be scared to sing in front of a bunch of people, too." She looked at Agatha. In a way, she wanted to tell Brenda about Agatha's singing, but she didn't want to spoil that part of the surprise. Boy, was everyone going to be amazed when they did their play! She grinned just thinking about it.

"We have to go," Brenda blurted.

"Oh, not yet," Cassie said, reaching for another cookie. "We haven't finished our tea. Isn't this rose-hip tea good?"

"Yes, but I told my mother I wouldn't be gone long," Brenda argued.

"Okay. We'll go in a minute." Cassie bit into her cookie. "These cookies are super. Did you make them from scratch?"

"Mm-hmm," Agatha said. "Granny was mixing them up when I got home. Then I helped bake them. We always bake. Every week we make cookies."

"My mom and I used to," Cassie said. "Now she gets the slice-and-bake kind once in a while, but she hardly ever has time anymore."

"Maybe you could bake with us sometime," Agatha suggested.

"Yes, that would be nice," her grandmother added. "What kind do you like best, dear?"

"We used to make peanut butter cookies," Cassie said. "I like those."

"Me, too!" Agatha grinned. "These are snickerdoodles." She indicated the plate. "They're Granny's favorite."

Cassie picked up another one. "Ummm! They're good, too. I like the cinnamon."

"Come on, Cassie. I'm all finished, and we have to go," Brenda said, standing up from the table.

Reluctantly, Cassie pushed back her chair. "Thank you for the tea and cookies," she said.

"Yes, thank you," said Brenda. "Now come on."

"You are welcome," said Mrs. Gifford. "We'll have to have that baking day real soon, Cassie."

"Yes," Agatha agreed eagerly. "That'll be fun!"

"I'd like that, and we'll work on our project tomorrow. Okay? I just can't today. I have to go with Brenda. . . ."

"Okay," Agatha said. Cassie could see that she was disappointed. How do I get myself into these messes? Cassie thought.

Brenda picked up her pack. "Come on," she urged, tugging at Cassie's sleeve.

"Thanks for letting us hear the music box again," Cassie said as Brenda pulled her to the door.

"Certainly, dear. You are very welcome," said Mrs. Gifford. She looked around to the chest where she had set her treasured box. "Why, where is it?"

"You put it on the chest," said Agatha.

"Yes, that's what I thought," her grandmother said. She stood up and carefully examined the whole top of the chest. "But it's not here now."

"Agatha had it the last time we saw it," Brenda said. "Didn't she, Cassie?"

Cassie looked uncertain.

"While you were out getting the flowers, she picked

it up, and we both saw her. Didn't we, Cassie?"

Cassie nodded.

"That's just because you were going to play it," said Agatha. "I put it right back."

"I didn't see you," Brenda said.

"I put it back," Agatha repeated.

"Maybe you put it someplace else by mistake," Cassie suggested.

"Yes," said Brenda. "Maybe that's what happened. It's probably here someplace, but we have to go. If I don't get home soon, my mom is really going to be mad. Come on, Cassie." Pulling her friend through the door with her, she closed it behind them and hurried down the steps, through the garden and out to the sidewalk.

Brenda walked so fast that Cassie had trouble keeping up with her. Neither said a word until they were almost at Brenda's house. "What a weird place!" she said. "I don't know who is worse, that stupid Aggy or her crazy old grandmother."

"I don't think they're so bad," Cassie said quietly. "They were just trying to be nice." She followed Brenda into her bedroom, wishing she could start the afternoon over and do it differently. What a mistake to think that Brenda and Agatha could be friends!

Brenda shoved her pack into the closet and closed the door. "Want to go up to the fort now?"

Cassie sank down on the bed and rubbed her hand over the spread. "I don't think so," she said. "I don't really feel like playing anything. I think I'll just go home."

"If that's what you want, go ahead." Brenda flopped onto a big pillow in the corner.

Cassie stood up. "I'll see you tomorrow, okay?"

"Okay," Brenda answered.

Cassie walked slowly toward home. When she came to the Gifford house, she turned up the walk and knocked at the door. Agatha answered. "Did you find it?" Cassie asked.

Agatha shook her head. "It's not here. She took it."

"Are you sure it's not here? It must be here someplace. Did you look everyplace?"

"Everyplace. Brenda Bolter took it," Agatha said with certainty.

"No, she didn't. She's my best friend. She wouldn't do anything like that. I know she wouldn't. It must be hidden someplace. Maybe she hid it for a joke or something."

"That wouldn't be a funny joke. Besides, we already looked for it everywhere."

"Let's look some more," Cassie insisted. "Come on. I'll help." She walked into the house and saw Mrs. Gifford sitting in the big rocking chair. Slowly rocking back and forth. She didn't look up at first.

"Cassie's back, Granny," Agatha said. "She wants to help us look."

"You can look if you want, but it's not here," the old woman said. She rocked back and forth in the creaky old chair.

Cassie started looking under the pillows and behind the plants. "We have to find it for her," she whispered. She looked in every corner of the living room,

then started down the hall toward the dining room.

Agatha followed her. "We already looked in there," she said again and again. "We already looked everywhere. We even took all the stuff out of the drawers and everything."

Indeed, the tablecloths, napkins and other contents of the chest were strewn about the room. Cassie went through everything anyway. She searched the dining room and the kitchen, then went back through the dining room and into the living room with Agatha behind her.

"I told you it's not here. Brenda stole it," Agatha said again.

Cassie turned to face her. "Stop saying that! She didn't steal it! I know she didn't! She's my friend."

"Well, she's not mine," Agatha retorted. "She doesn't like me, and if she didn't take Granny's music box, then where is it?"

Even with the girls shouting at one another right in front of her, Mrs. Gifford didn't say a word. She just rocked back and forth in that chair. It gave Cassie a creepy feeling. She looked from the silent woman to the girl.

"She stole it," Agatha said again, pursing her lips together in a determined expression.

"No, she didn't!" Cassie shouted. "I know she didn't, and I think you're horrible to say she did. You're a horrible liar, and I don't ever want to come here again. I don't want to bake cookies with you, and I don't want to do that stupid puppet play!"

She ran out and let the door slam behind her.

At home, Cassie went straight to her room and picked up her little bear. She stroked the soft fur on the top of his head and held him up to look her in the eye. "I don't ever want to lose you, PeeWee," she said. "Not ever, ever, ever, even when I'm an old lady."

Holding PeeWee close, she sat on the edge of her bed, rocking back and forth and thinking of Mrs. Gifford. "I know Brenda didn't take it," she whispered. "I know she didn't."

Cassie was still in her room when her mother got home from work. She poked her head in the door. "Hi, sweetie," she said.

"Hi, Mom," Cassie answered.

"Pretty quiet around here today. How do you feel?" Mrs. Bowen walked over and put a hand on Cassie's forehead.

"Fine," Cassie said.

"Are you sure? Joel is coming down with a terrible cold. I think he has a fever. I hope you aren't getting it, too."

"I'm not, Mom," Cassie said. "I just had a rotten day."

"This morning you were all excited about making those puppets. Didn't you have a good time?"

"Not exactly," Cassie said. "We never got to work on them. Then Mrs. Gifford's music box got lost, and she's real sad. No one can find it."

"That's too bad," her mother said. "But I'm sure it'll turn up. Those things always do. I'd better get your brother some aspirin and start dinner if we're ever going to eat." Ruffling Cassie's hair and giving her a little cheer-up smile, she hustled out of the room.

Cassie sighed and flopped back down on her bed. "Sure," she said to herself. "It'll turn up." But inside, she wasn't one bit convinced.

Secret in the Fort

Brenda didn't mention the Giffords or the music box the next morning, and Cassie didn't either. When they got to school, Agatha, in a dress again, was in her corner by the fence. Cassie tried not to look at her as she and Brenda entered the school yard, but she could feel Agatha watching her as they walked across the playground. It felt as if Agatha's eyes were burning a hole right through her.

After lunch, Mr. Garner gave them time to work on their plays. Cassie and Agatha took their books into the corner behind the science shelf. Cassie opened her book and stared at it. Agatha watched her for a while; then she opened her book, too.

Once Mr. Garner came by and asked, "How's it going?"

"Okay," Cassie said.

He looked from one girl to the other. "You sure? You have to be ready next week, you know. Just a few days left."

"I know," said Cassie.

Mr. Garner looked at Agatha. She nodded at him.

"Well, then." He shrugged. "Just let me know if you need any help." He moved off to the front of the room, where John and Curtis had started shouting at one another.

"Why didn't you tell him?" Agatha asked.

"Tell him what?"

"You know. That you don't want to be my partner anymore."

Cassie shrugged. "Maybe it's none of his business." She went back to staring at her book.

After school, she walked to the corner with Brenda and Sylvia, but she didn't say much. Sylvia was going over to Brenda's to work on their project, and the two of them laughed and joked as usual. Cassie was glad that at least they didn't say anything about Agatha or her grandmother, even though they could see Agatha way up ahead of them. Mostly Cassie thought about what it would be like next week when she had to tell Mr. Garner she wasn't going to do any play.

When she got home, Joel was watching TV. He had stayed home because of his cold. Cassie deliberately walked between her brother and the television set. He didn't even yell at her. She stopped in front of him, but he just moved his head so he could see around her. So she went on into her room.

She picked up her pillow and threw it on the floor. She kicked it against the wall and flopped down on her bed. She stared at PeeWee, but he just stared back. She flipped through a book, tossed it aside, pushed herself to her feet and looked at her reflection in the mirror. Another rotten day. That's what it was. In fact, her whole life was pretty rotten. She stuck out her tongue at the face in the mirror, which rudely returned the gesture.

With a sigh, she shuffled out to the kitchen, where she poured herself a glass of milk. She only drank half of it. Milk wasn't reaching the empty feeling inside. She rested her chin on her hands and sat staring at the white liquid left in the glass.

"Hey, Cassie! Get me some orange juice, would you?" Joel called from the living room.

"Get it yourself," she called back. "You're not dying."

"A lot you'd care if I were," he said, coming into the kitchen.

"So? You'd care if I were dead. You'd be glad. You wouldn't have to look out for me anymore." She stuck her tongue out at him as she retreated into the living room. "Everybody would be glad," she muttered under her breath.

Joel was watching some science fiction movie. Cassie changed the channel.

"Hey! I was watching that!" Joel stormed into the room and changed it back.

"I hate science fiction," Cassie complained.

"So what! Nobody said you have to watch it."

"You always get to watch what you want."

"Look, kid, it just so happens that this time I was watching first. I also happen to be sick, and I need my rest, so if you don't mind, why don't you go find something else to do?"

"There isn't anything except television, but I hate your stupid shows."

"Boy, you're in a great mood! Why don't you go over to Brenda's and pick on her for a change."

"She's working on her school thing with Sylvia again, and anyway, maybe I don't feel like going out. This is my house, too, you know!"

"So stay here, but shut up so I can watch the movie," Joel ordered.

Cassie put her feet on the coffee table. She wasn't supposed to do that. Mom would get mad if she knew, but Joel just ignored her. She pushed one of the sofa cushions onto the floor. He ignored that, too. Cassie glared at him. "Okay! I'll go see if they've finished yet." She grabbed her sweater and marched out the door, giving it a good hard slam.

She took the long way around to Brenda's to avoid going by the Gifford house. She wasn't in any hurry. When she got there, she stood on the sidewalk and watched Brenda's bedroom window. She couldn't tell if they were in there or not.

They were probably still busy. Even if they weren't, they probably wouldn't want her butting in anyway. Sylvia wouldn't, especially. Sylvia liked having Brenda all to herself.

Cassie sat down on the curb and picked up a handful of pebbles. One at a time, she threw them at the toe of her sneaker. She only missed once, but it was an easy target. She stood up, brushed off the seat of her jeans and headed up toward the fort.

Several feet from the fort, Cassie stopped. She heard voices coming from inside. She turned and took a few quick steps down the hill. She was going to go tell Brenda about the intruders right away. Brenda wouldn't mind being interrupted for something as important as this. She and Brenda would show whoever was in there whose fort this was!

But then she decided to get a little more information first. She would do the detective work on her own, and then they could make a good plan. Brenda and Sylvia would be impressed.

She inched her way back up the hill, careful not to make a sound. Whoever was in there was having a good time. They were laughing. She climbed closer and stopped to listen again.

Brenda! It was Brenda and Sylvia!

Cassie clenched her fists and felt her jaw tighten. Brenda had Sylvia in the fort, *their* fort, without her! Without even asking her! She crept closer, stopping just outside the doorway.

Brenda was talking in a squeaky, high-pitched voice. "When I was a little girl, I was in a play and I was a lovely fairy, and I danced in front of all the lovely people, dearie, and it was all so lovely."

Sylvia giggled.

"Would you like some of my special brew, dear?" Brenda went on. "It's so lovely that you came over." Both girls burst into laughter again.

Cassie was about to open the curtain and tell Brenda how mad she was when she heard something else. Something that made her feet freeze to the spot and put a hard, cold lump in her stomach. It sounded just like ... it couldn't be ... it sounded exactly like Mrs. Gifford's music box!

Cassie threw back the curtain. Two surprised faces turned to look at her as Brenda snatched something off the table and hid it behind her back.

"What do you want?" Sylvia said.

"This is my fort," Cassie responded. "Mine and Brenda's. I have a right to be here."

"So do I. Brenda said I could come. She invited me," Sylvia said.

"It's all right, Cassie," Brenda said soothingly. "I'm glad you came over. We were just about to call you. Weren't we, Sylvia? We just finished our work, and I was going to go in and call you."

Cassie stepped to the left, trying to see the object Brenda had concealed behind her, but Brenda turned, keeping it carefully hidden.

"Why don't we all go on in the house and get something to drink?" she suggested.

"I'm not thirsty," Cassie said.

"Well, how about if we go play my new game or something?" Brenda offered.

"Yes. Good idea. Let's go," agreed Sylvia.

"Go ahead. I'm not stopping you," Cassie said curtly.

"No. I mean all of us," Brenda insisted.

"Okay. You go get the game, and I'll just wait here," Cassie said.

"I don't want to bring it out here. It might get dirty," Brenda argued.

"We've played with stuff out here before," Cassie said.

"She's just being a brat," Sylvia said. "Probably because she's been spending so much time with Agatha Gifford."

Brenda turned to look at Sylvia. Cassie stepped quickly behind her. Brenda spun around, but it was too late. Cassie had seen it. It was definitely Mrs. Gifford's music box.

"You did take it!" she burst out, still unable to believe Brenda would do such a thing.

"Take what?" Brenda said innocently. "I didn't take anything."

"Yes, you did! The music box! You have it! I saw it! You stole Mrs. Gifford's music box!"

"I did not!"

"You've got it right there in your hands. I said you didn't take it, but you did! I even called Agatha a liar!"

"She is a liar. If she said I stole it, she is."

"Okay. If you didn't take it, then how did it get here?"

"It just probably got in my stuff by mistake."

"How could it get in there by mistake?" Cassie said hotly.

"How should I know?"

"Maybe Agatha put it in there to try to get Brenda in trouble," Sylvia said.

"Sure. That's probably what happened," Brenda agreed. "She just wanted to get me in trouble."

"Why would she do a dumb thing like that?" Cassie asked.

"Because she's a dumb girl, that's why," Sylvia said.

"Yes," said Brenda. "Real dumb!"

Cassie looked Brenda straight in the eye, wanting to believe what her friend was saying, but knowing in her heart it wasn't true. Agatha might dress differently. She might not smile at school. She might even want to do something to get back at Brenda and some of the others for being so mean. Cassie wouldn't blame her if she did. But Agatha would never do something like that.

"She's not dumb, and she's not mean either. Even if she wanted to be mean to you, she wouldn't be that mean to her grandmother. She wouldn't take her grandmother's music box," Cassie said firmly. "You're a liar. A thief and a liar."

"She is not!" Sylvia said. "You are! You're just as dumb as Agatha. You think you're so perfect. Maybe Brenda just wanted to have a little fun!"

"That's right," Brenda said. "What's wrong with having some fun?"

"It's not fun for Mrs. Gifford," Cassie said.

"So? Who cares about that crazy old witch?" Brenda retorted.

"She probably wants to learn to be a witch herself," Sylvia said. "Maybe she's already taking lessons. She probably wants to be best friends with that stupid Saggy Aggy."

"Mrs. Gifford isn't a witch!" Cassie shouted. "And it's Agatha, not Saggy Aggy! And she's not stupid, either.

She's not stupid enough to steal something that doesn't belong to her!"

"I told you I didn't steal it," Brenda insisted.

"Then how did it get here?"

"How should I know? Just by mistake, or else Agatha did it, like Sylvia said."

"Okay. If it was just by mistake, then why don't you take it back?" Cassie said.

"Why should I? She's just a crazy old lady," said Brenda.

"It's really special to her," Cassie pleaded more gently. "She had it for such a long time, and she said it was the last present her father gave her. Now she's sad without it. Really, really sad."

"I don't care," Brenda said.

"But she's really sad," Cassie repeated.

"So?"

"So you have to give it back."

"Who says?"

"Yes, who says, Miss Goody-goody?" Sylvia said.

Cassie shot her a dirty look and turned back to Brenda. "Just give it to me, and I'll take it back," she offered.

Brenda clutched the box. "What'll you tell her?"

"She doesn't have to do what you say!" Sylvia said.

"Right! I don't have to mind you! You're not my mother!" Brenda said.

"If you don't give it back, I'll go tell your mother," Cassie said.

"You will not."

"Yes, I will."

"Stupid tattletale," Sylvia said.

Cassie looked directly into Brenda's eyes. "I will if you don't give it back."

"Go ahead," Brenda said defiantly, "but if you do, we'll never be friends again. Ever."

Cassie stared at Brenda.

"Anyway, she won't believe you," Brenda added.

Looking at the music box in Brenda's hands, Cassie thought about Mrs. Gifford in the rocking chair. She thought about the lonely, hurt look in Agatha's eyes, too. That look was more heartbreaking than the sad, dull look she had when the others teased her. What if they never smiled again, either one of them, Agatha or her grandmother? What if they stayed that sad forever? Cassie looked at the box. Somehow she had to get it back to them.

She looked at Brenda, then at Sylvia. They glared back. She couldn't fight the two of them. Slowly Cassie turned and took a step toward the door. But instead of going out, she whirled back, catching the others by surprise. In a quick move, she snatched the precious music box from Brenda's hands and dashed through the door.

"Get her!" Sylvia yelled.

Cassie heard them behind her. She could tell they were close as she ran down the hill, clinging tightly to Mrs. Gifford's treasure and trying desperately not to lose her balance. Her heart pounded in her chest.

Their footsteps were right on her heels; then she heard a skidding sound and a scream. Loose dirt and rocks tumbled past her down the slope. One of them must have fallen. Cassie didn't dare stop or look back.

"Go ahead!" Brenda screamed. "Go ahead, tattletale, but I'm never going to speak to you again! Never! I mean it!"

"Witch!" Sylvia yelled. "Stupid little witch-lover!"

"Witch-lover!" Brenda echoed. "I'm never going to be your friend again as long as I live." She was crying.

Cassie ran on. She didn't stop until she got to the sidewalk, where she glanced back at them. Brenda was holding her knee, and Sylvia had an arm around her.

Cassie took off down the street and didn't stop until she was well out of their sight. She slowed down to catch her breath, listening and glancing back over her shoulder in case they continued the chase. Her heart pounded fast and hard, and Brenda's words echoed in her head. "I'm never going to be your friend again as long as I live . . . never . . ."

Tears spilled from her eyes and ran down her cheeks. Cassie looked at the music box in her hands through the watery haze and wondered if it was really worth it.

Making It Right

Cassie walked slowly toward the Gifford house carrying the music box. Maybe, she thought, it wasn't too late to take it back to Brenda. She could go back and tell her she was sorry. If she waited until Sylvia was gone, she might be able to convince Brenda that taking it was wrong.

She could tell her about Mrs. Gifford in the rocking chair. Maybe when Brenda realized how important it was, she'd take it back herself, and everything would be all right. Mrs. Gifford would have her music box, Agatha would be happy to see her grandmother happy and Cassie and Brenda could be friends again. Cassie Bowen and Brenda Bolter, best friends forever.

Anyway, there was the problem of what she would tell Mrs. Gifford. Agatha and her grandmother might think she was the one who took it.

And how could she face Agatha after calling her a liar? She'd called Agatha a liar and then found out that her best friend was a thief. Everything was so mixed up. Nothing was right! Maybe nothing would ever be right again.

Cassie wished she'd watched television with her brother instead of going up to the fort. She wished she hadn't found Brenda with the music box. She wished she hadn't gotten herself mixed up in the whole mess.

But wishing wouldn't do her any good. She *was* mixed up in it. It was her idea to take Brenda to the Giffords' house in the first place. It was her idea to show Brenda the music box. None of this would have happened if it weren't for her. It was all her fault, and now here she was with the stupid thing in her hands.

Her head thumped as she stopped and looked at the music box. What should she do? Giving it back to Brenda wasn't right, but if she took it back to the Giffords', they might accuse her of being the thief. Somehow she had to get rid of it.

She clutched it as she trudged on with heavy steps. Just ahead, she saw a lawn surrounded by a tall, thick hedge. It gave her an idea. As she approached the hedge, she took a quick look behind her. She looked in the windows of the nearby houses, too. No one was in sight. Quickly she stooped and slipped the music box deep under the bushes. Standing up, she took another look around and walked on down the street.

Cassie made her plans as she walked. She would leave a note in Agatha's desk at school, telling her where to find the music box. She would disguise her handwriting. Neither Agatha nor her grandmother would ever have to know she had anything to do with it. Maybe later she could tell Brenda, so she would know she wasn't a tattletale. It might work out just fine, as long as somebody else didn't come along and find it first.

It was Friday. No more school until Monday. That was a long time. What if somebody else did find it and didn't know whose it was? What if they just thought it was finders keepers? Had she hidden it well enough, or might somebody see it if they just happened to walk by? What if Sylvia found it on her way home? She'd never give it back. Besides, what if it rained during the night?

Cassie turned around and went back to the hedge. Just walking by, she couldn't see the music box. Trying not to look too suspicious, she pretended that she had dropped something and got down on her hands and knees to pick it up.

Maybe it would be better to leave it on Mrs. Gifford's front porch. She could knock on the door and run off, or maybe open the lid and leave it playing. When Agatha and Mrs. Gifford heard it playing, they would come out and find it, but she'd be gone, and they'd never know who put it there.

Cassie reached under the hedge and pulled out the music box. Sitting there on the sidewalk, she gently opened the lid. The little golden bird began to dance and sing. As she listened, Cassie wondered if Mrs. Gifford was still rocking in that chair, rocking and staring as she was the day before.

Listening to the little bird sing and thinking about Mrs. Gifford, Cassie knew what she had to do. Maybe she couldn't make it right with Brenda or with Agatha, but she could make sure Mrs. Gifford got her music box back safely. She could make that part right, at least.

She stood up and walked on with determination. She walked on until she came to Mrs. Gifford's beautiful flower garden; then she turned, walked directly to the porch and up the steps. She knocked on the door of the old house. Cassie thought she could hear the faint creaking of the rocking chair, but she might have imagined it. She heard no other sounds. No one came to the door.

She knocked again. Louder. To her ears, it sounded like thunder. Then she heard footsteps, and Agatha opened the door. Cassie pushed the music box into the surprised girl's hands. "I . . . I found this," she said and, turning around, ran down the steps, back to the sidewalk and up the street.

She ran until she was inside her own house, in her own room, where she collapsed across her bed. She pulled the pillow over her head, but she couldn't shut out the horrible sounds of Brenda's and Sylvia's voices. "Witch-lover! Stupid witch! Never be friends again! Never be friends again! Witch-lover!" she heard over and over.

And then her own voice calling Agatha a liar. "Liar! Liar! Liar!"

And Sylvia and Brenda saying, "Tattletale! Stupid tattletale!"

She pulled PeeWee close and buried her face in his soft fur. "I guess you're the only friend I've got now," she sobbed. "I guess you're the only friend I'll ever have, but I'm not a tattletale. No matter what they say, I didn't tell on her." Cassie pulled the blankets over herself, curled up with her bear and let the tears come.

Never Again

Cassie cried herself to sleep. She was still sleeping when her mother came home. Mrs. Bowen sat on the edge of the bed and put a hand on Cassie's forehead. Cassie rolled over and looked up at her mother.

"How do you feel, sweetheart?" Mrs. Bowen asked. "I was afraid you'd get this cold Joel has. I thought you were coming down with it last night. I should have had you stay home today, too."

Cassie shook her head. "I'm not sick, Mom. Just tired." Her mother smoothed back her hair.

"Well, at least tomorrow is Saturday. You'll be able to stay home and rest. Maybe you'll feel better by Monday."

Cassie couldn't imagine that she'd ever feel better. She certainly didn't ever want to go back to school.

"You know, Cassie, I did have one idea today, about this summer, I mean," Mrs. Bowen went on. "Mrs. Gifford is home almost all the time, and now that you and her granddaughter are friends, I was thinking that I might ask her to keep an eye on you this summer."

Cassie's stomach jumped. "I don't need a baby-sitter, Mom," she protested, her face growing hot as she fought back the tears.

"I know that, sweetheart. I don't mean like a real baby-sitter. Just someone to be there when you need something and, well, just keep an eye on things. I think I'll call her and talk about it."

Cassie panicked at the thought of her mother talking to Mrs. Gifford. She could just imagine what the old woman would say. Certainly she would never want Cassie in her house again, not after all that had happened. Then Mom would be upset, and everything would get even worse. She frantically searched her mind for a way to stop that call as her mother went on talking.

"You seemed to enjoy going over there this week. She's very nice, isn't she? I imagine she can use the money, too. Of course I can't pay much, but you won't be much trouble. Tomorrow we can walk over and talk to them."

"No!" Cassie wailed. "No! We can't go over there. And you can't call her either!" The tears she'd been struggling to hold back rolled down her cheeks.

Mrs. Bowen was surprised by the intensity of Cassie's outburst. "I . . . I'm sorry," she said, putting an arm around her daughter's shoulders. "I thought you liked them."

"I did," Cassie sobbed. "I mean, I do. They're very nice, but I don't think they like me. Not anymore."

"Of course they do," her mother soothed. Cassie resisted her attempts to pull her close.

"No, they don't. Not after . . . what I did. I took Brenda there, and she stole Mrs. Gifford's music box that she had since she was a little girl, and Agatha said Brenda did it, and I said she was a liar, and I wouldn't do the puppet play with her." Cassie collapsed into her mother's arms and sobbed.

Mrs. Bowen held her, smoothing her hair and gently rocking back and forth on the edge of the bed. She let Cassie cry for a few moments.

"And now Brenda will never be my friend again either," Cassie sobbed. "She and Sylvia said I'm a tattletale, but I'm not. I just gave it back."

"You gave the music box back to Mrs. Gifford?" her mother asked.

"Yes. I had to, because Mrs. Gifford was so sad. Her music box was so special to her," Cassie said, sniffling. "I didn't think Brenda would take it. I thought she'd see how nice Agatha and her grandmother are. I thought we could all be friends. I really didn't think Brenda took it, but I went to the fort, and she had it in there."

"Brenda had the music box in the fort?"

"Yes, and I told her she should take it back, but she wouldn't, so I grabbed it away and ran. Brenda and Sylvia called me names, but I had to take it. I just had to get it back for Mrs. Gifford. Her papa gave it to her when she was a little girl." Cassie glanced at her bear lying on the pillow.

"Oh, my poor baby," her mother said. "What a hard

time you've had, but do you know what? I'm very proud of you. I'm glad that you did the best thing, even though Brenda wouldn't. Even though the other girls got mad at you. Maybe you are more mature and can handle things better than I thought."

Hearing her mother say those words was some consolation to Cassie. She was glad she had returned the music box. At least someone was happy with her, even if she didn't have any friends now.

"Why do you think Brenda would take Mrs. Gifford's music box?" Mrs. Bowen asked.

"I don't know. She just likes to show off sometimes. Now she always wants to play with Sylvia. They're always showing off and acting smart."

"Sounds like you are upset with Brenda about a lot of things."

"Sometimes she's mean. She and Sylvia and some other girls call Agatha names. They call her Saggy Aggy and Thrifty Gifford and stuff like that, and they laugh right in her face."

"Did you do that, too?"

Cassie hung her head. "I never said it, but I never said anything nice either. Not till Mr. Garner made us be partners. At first, I didn't even want to be her partner."

"Do you know what I think?" Mrs. Bowen said, lifting Cassie's chin to look at her. "I think Mr. Garner chose a very good person to be a partner for a new girl."

"Agatha's really nice. She understands about things, but now everything is spoiled," Cassie said. Fresh tears wet her cheeks. "Now we can't be partners, and we can't do the play."

"Why not? You said you took the music box back."

"I did."

"What did they say?"

"Nothing. I just gave it to Agatha and left."

"Maybe they aren't upset with you. How about if we call and go talk to them about it?" Mrs. Bowen suggested.

"No," Cassie said. "I took Brenda there, and she took the music box. It's all my fault, and I don't want to talk about it. None of them will ever be my friend again, never ever."

"Never is a very long time, Cassie," her mother said. "People do change. Sometimes for the better, sometimes not. Brenda may get tired of Sylvia and her unpleasant ways. If she doesn't, I'm sure you'll make lots of other friends. And I'll just bet that Agatha and her grandmother would like to be two of them."

"No, they wouldn't," Cassie said. "They'll never like me again. None of them will."

Cassie was glad the next day was Saturday. She spent the whole weekend inside, sitting in her room or watching television.

She looked through her closet, too. Some of those dresses really were pretty. She even tried on a couple of them. What would happen if she did wear one to school?

Friends

Cassie didn't feel like going to school on Monday morning, but since she wasn't sick, her mother insisted. Cassie thought that having no friends was just about the worst sickness in the world.

She took out one of the dresses she had tried on. It was pretty, and it would be cooler than pants. Besides, she really didn't have anything to lose. It wouldn't matter what she wore. But she put it back and put on her jeans, ate a few bites of breakfast and started toward school.

She didn't bother to wait for Brenda on the corner, but walked the whole way alone. Even with her dawdling over her clothes, she was there early. She could tell, because there were hardly any kids on the playground.

She slammed a tetherball with her fist as she went by.

"Play you," Stacy called, running up to the pole.

Cassie shook her head and kept walking. She went to the drinking fountain and took a swallow of water before wandering to the main building. She sat on the steps and watched the kids coming into the school yard.

She still couldn't see Brenda anywhere. She wondered if Brenda might be looking for her on their corner after all, and began to wish she had waited, just in case. She hoped Brenda wouldn't be late because of her.

Agatha came through the gate. She had on her jeans again. Biting her lip, Cassie opened the book on her lap and tried to look busy.

When she looked up again, Agatha was standing in her usual place by the fence. She could tell that Agatha was watching her. She saw her move her hand a little bit. It might have been a wave, but maybe not. Cassie wasn't sure. Agatha did seem to be smiling, though, just a little bit.

Cassie squirmed uncomfortably on the step. She looked down at her book.

When Cassie looked up toward Agatha again, someone was blocking her view. Brenda and Sylvia were standing right in front of her.

"Well, if it isn't the tattletale," Sylvia jeered.

Brenda looked at Cassie without saying anything.

"How are the witch lessons going?" Sylvia asked mockingly. She poked Brenda with an elbow and laughed.

"Come on," Brenda said. "I don't want to talk to a witch-lover."

"Right. Who wants to talk to a tattletale witch?" Sylvia said over her shoulder as she and Brenda headed for the four-square game.

"I'm no tattletale," Cassie muttered under her breath

as they walked off, "and I'm not a thief or a liar either." She felt a stinging behind her eyes and blinked to keep back the tears. She bent over her book and stared at it hard. Their teasing never made Agatha cry, and it wasn't going to make her cry either. Not here, where they could see and tease her more.

She turned a page and tried to pretend that she didn't care about anything except the story she wasn't even reading. She felt a hand softly touch her sleeve and looked up to see Agatha standing next to her.

"I . . ." Agatha began hesitantly. "Granny said to thank you for bringing the music box back."

Cassie looked from Agatha to the fence. "That's okay," she said. "I just found it . . . someplace. Is she okay now? Is she happy again?"

Agatha nodded. "She's fine, now that she has her music box."

"That's good," Cassie said. "I'm glad." She saw Sylvia point at her and whisper something to Brenda. Brenda turned to look at her, and both of them laughed.

Agatha saw them, too. "You just have to ignore them," she said quietly. "Just don't pay any attention."

Cassie sat staring straight ahead. For several minutes, Agatha stood beside her, neither of them speaking. Finally Agatha turned and started back toward the fence. Cassie watched her go for a while before she stood up. "Wait a minute," she called, walking over to her.

Agatha faced her.

"I was just thinking . . ." Cassie began. "I was thinking maybe we could still do that puppet show . . . if you want to."

"Do you?" Agatha asked timidly.

"Mr. Garner's going to be plenty mad if we don't," Cassie said.

"Yes," Agatha agreed. "I guess we'd really better."

"Maybe . . . do you think it would be all right if we worked on the puppets after school today? I mean, at your house?"

Agatha smiled and nodded. "I think that would be just fine."

"Your grandmother won't mind . . . if I come?"

Agatha shook her head. "She'll be glad," she insisted. "She likes you."

Cassie blushed nervously and shifted her book from one arm to the other. She surveyed the playground and spotted an available tetherball pole. "Want to play tetherball or something?" she asked.

"Okay." Agatha smiled.

"Those jeans really do look good on you," Cassie said as they walked toward the tetherball pole.

"Thanks," Agatha said.

"You know, I have some neat dresses my cousin Lisa sent. Maybe one of these days we could both wear dresses," Cassie suggested.

Agatha nodded. "That would be fun sometimes."

They were passing near the four-square court when Sylvia spotted them again. "Hey, look!" she shouted. "It's Saggy Aggy and Goody Tattletale, the two witches!"

"Hey, witches! What do you think this is? Halloween?" Brenda hooted.

Cassie cringed and walked faster, but to her surprise, Agatha turned around and stuck her tongue out at them.

Cassie stared at her in amazement, and even the other girls were left momentarily speechless. Agatha shrugged. A smile spread slowly across her face.

"I'm sorry I called you a liar," Cassie said.

"That's okay," Agatha said. "Sometimes you have to stick up for your friends."

"Yes, sometimes you do," Cassie said. Quietly she slipped her arm through Agatha's as they walked on across the playground.

About the Author

ANNA GROSSNICKLE HINES says that *Cassie Bowen Takes Witch Lessons* came to her in a dream. "The plot and characters were all there. The story has been through many revisions but remains basically the one I dreamed."

Mrs. Hines has written and illustrated picture books for younger children, including *Maybe a Band-Aid Will Help, Come to the Meadow,* and *Bethany for Real.* She lives in Twain Harte, California, with her husband and three daughters.